Eyewitness

OTHER BOOKS BY
MARGARET THOMPSON

Squaring the Round:
The Early Days of Fort St. James
(1992) — prose & poetry

Hide and Seek
(Caitlin Press, 1996)
short stories

Eyewitness

Margaret Thompson

RONSDALE PRESS

RONSDALE PRESS
3350 West 21st Avenue
Vancouver, B.C., Canada
V6S 1G7

Set in Minion: 12 pt on 16
Typesetting: Julie Cochrane
Printing: Hignell Printing, Winnipeg, Manitoba
Cover Art: Elaine Cuttler
Cover Design: Julie Cochrane

Ronsdale Press wishes to thank the Canada Council for the Arts, the Government of Canada through the Book Publishing Industry Development Program (BPIDP), and the Province of British Columbia through the British Columbia Arts Council for their support of its publishing program.

CANADIAN CATALOGUING IN PUBLICATION DATA
Thompson, Margaret, 1940 Nov. 5–
    Eyewitness

    ISBN 0-921870-74-4

    1. Fort St. James (B.C.) — Juvenile fiction. 2. Carrier Indians — Juvenile fiction. I. Title.
PS8589.H5228E93 2000   jC813'.54   C99-911296-1
PZ7.T37164Ey 2000

*For Zachary and Grace
and all those who ever wonder what
it was like back then.*

*With special thanks to
Nellie Dionne for her help with
the Carrier language.*

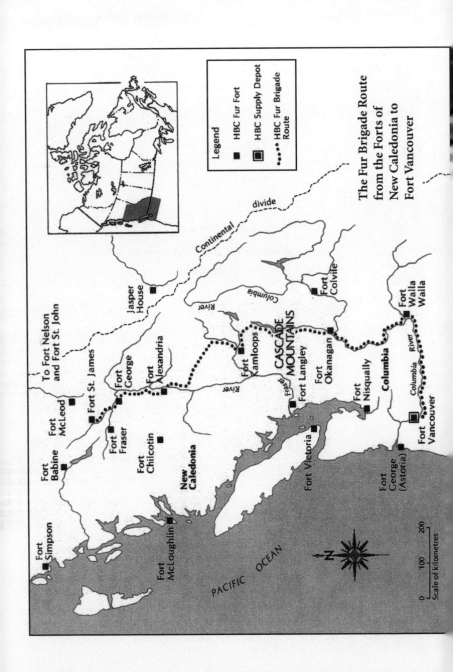

Legend
■ HBC Fur Fort
▣ HBC Supply Depot
•••• HBC Fur Brigade Route

The Fur Brigade Route
from the Forts of
New Caledonia to
Fort Vancouver

Continental divide

Fort Simpson
Fort Babine
Fort McLeod
Fort St. James
To Fort Nelson and Fort St. John
Fort Fraser
Fort George
Fort Alexandria
Jasper House
Fort McLoughlin
Fort Chilcotin
New Caledonia
Fort Kamloops
CASCADE MOUNTAINS
Columbia River
Fort Colvile
Fraser River
Fort Langley
Fort Okanagan
Fort Walla Walla
Fort Victoria
Fort Nisqually
Columbia
Columbia River
Fort George (Astoria)
Fort Vancouver

PACIFIC OCEAN

N

0   100   200
Scale of kilometres

PREFACE

The Hudson's Bay Company is, of course, a real commercial enterprise and its place in the history of the development of Canada and British Columbia a matter of record.

There is still a Fort at Fort St. James. The buildings are not the ones Peter would have known; the Fort has been rebuilt several times in its nearly two-hundred-year history. It is now a National Historic Site maintained by Parks Canada and restored to the way it was in 1896.

Many of the events in the story actually happened — the murders during Mr. Yale's absence, the killing of the two murderers, the confrontation in the tradestore, the rescue of James Douglas by his wife, the visit of the Governor, to name just a few.

Chief Kwah was a real person. His grave house still stands at the edge of Stuart Lake near the outlet to the river. James Douglas is a brash young Clerk in the story but he went on to become Sir James Douglas, the first Governor of the brand new province of British Columbia.

John Yale, James McDougall and William Connolly were all Officers of the Company and served at Fort St. James. Sir George Simpson was the powerful Governor. Waccan did come with Simon Fraser and stay at the Fort as Interpreter until his death from measles many years later, when his son took on the same role.

Some of the women are also real. Amelia Douglas was the daughter of William Connolly and his "country wife" Suzanne, who was Cree. Nancy Boucher was the daughter of James McDougall.

Peter Mackenzie, Robert Finlay, the Benoîts, Gaston and Cadunda are not real, but they could be. The early history of the fur trade in British Columbia is peopled with expatriate Scots, French and Métis, and First Nations. Their lives were just as hard as the story suggests. The Europeans would probably not have survived in this vast, isolated land without the willing help of the Native people and their millennia of experience.

But from this remote place, its apparently insignificant inhabitants and their fight to survive and prosper came the westernmost province of all, and a Canada that finally stretched from sea to sea to sea. It truly was the beginning of great things.

ONE

❧

A Departure

Before I was seven years old, Misfortune tapped me on the shoulder and claimed me for his own.

At the time, the day seemed no different from a thousand others. I can remember stumbling out of bed in the darkness of a late winter morning when my father had silently shaken me awake, shivering uncontrollably as I dragged on stiff stockings and fur-lined moccasins and lifted my coat from the deer antler that served as a peg on the wall by my cot.

Impatiently my father pushed my dithering fingers aside and fastened the buttons for me, then motioned for me to pick up my fur cap and mittens. My mother had made them for me, my father had said in one of his rare talkative moments, and I clung to them, even though they were almost too small to be any more use, because they were all I had of her.

I could dimly remember a smiling face framed by a curtain of heavy black hair but even that was fading. I tried to imagine her bent over the small mittens in the candlelight, stitching the tiny beads and pieces of porcupine quill on the backs and trimming the cuffs with strips of rabbit fur, but the picture refused to stay still in my mind. My father's voice banished it.

"Stir yourself, Peter. There's work to be done and no time to waste woolgathering."

Obediently I followed my father out of our tiny room. Since my mother's death in the grim winter of 1821, when she fell victim to the measles that attacked me just as soon as we arrived at Fort St. James, my father had changed. His silence hung like a great weight over my head that might crash down at any moment. When he spoke I responded immediately as if to prevent that from happening.

From the corner of the kitchen I heard a soft rattling snore. The apprentice, David Murray, had a narrow wooden cot behind the table. I envied him, for he at least had the benefit of the fire in the little hearth while it burned. We froze behind the closed door of our room, and there was a hole in the parchment leather covering the window just by my cot. In a blizzard the flakes would trickle in like sand

and I would wake to find a little heap of snow lying on my quilt.

As we passed the hearth, my father rattled the poker in the ashes and flung another log on the embers, but we did not stay to watch the fire come to life. We went out into the darkness. The snow squeaked underfoot and I could feel the hairs in my nose freezing stiff.

A figure loomed out of the ghostly dark. It was Teluah, the Carrier Indian who often helped about the Fort. He was to be my father's companion on their trip to Fort Fraser to deliver some much-needed supplies.

The train had been packed the day before. The big sled was loaded with bags of flour, tobacco twist wrapped in linen and canvas, kegs of nails and moosehide. Our job now was to harness the dogs who would pull the train. One by one, as Teluah held them, I released the dogs who were going on the trip from the tethers that kept them apart and prevented fights. They all wanted to go. All of them were standing up, wide awake, their tails curled and wagging in anticipation. They yipped and howled and strained at the ropes, making it very hard to untie the knots. So great was their excitement at the prospect of action that I felt sorry for the ones who were not harnessed and attached to the traces on the sled. I knew just how they felt. I was being left behind, too.

The first light was diluting the sky as I helped Teluah clip the last dog to the harness. It was Vixen, my favourite, too small and wayward to be a lead dog, but full of heart and fire. I was rubbing her ears as my father turned to me. He gave me the stern, searching look I was so used to, and finally sighed and shook his head as if I represented a puzzle he could not solve.

"Away inside now," he said. "I'll be back in a week or so. Behave yourself and try not to be a burden."

Then he turned away, settled Teluah among the bundles, grasped the back of the sled and shouted encouragingly at the dogs. The polished runners hissed on the snow as the dogs plunged forward and the train slid down the gentle slope towards the frozen lake.

It was the last time I ever saw my father.

TWO

ᴑ

Alone in the World

The first intimation of trouble came at noon the same day. I had spent the time since Father's departure with Mrs. Benoît and her two small children. Mrs. Benoît was the wife of one of the middlemen or ordinary boatmen. She did most of the cooking and cleaning about the men's house.

She was round and soft, a little dumpling of a woman not all that much taller than I, kind in an absent-minded, general way. She was always busy, but I stayed near her because she loved to sing at her work and the kitchen always rang to the rollicking French songs she had learned as a child. Besides, if I got underfoot, she was not nearly as impatient or heavy-handed as the men.

I was watching her lift the heavy kettle of water onto a hook over the fire when the door opened and David Murray stamped in, blowing on his nails.

"Anything to eat yet?" he enquired with a grin.

Mrs. Benoît looked at him, her knife poised to cut into the dried salmon lying like a varnished orange board on the table.

"I give you the tail, you chew on that," she offered.

"Bah!" came the reply. "It's bad enough cooked."

"Then you wait, jus' like everybody else," said Mrs. Benoît.

David kicked off his boots and then glanced quickly at me before speaking again.

"Er, didn't Teluah leave with Mackenzie today?"

Mrs. Benoît nodded.

"That's what I thought," David went on, "only I could have sworn I saw him earlier, on the lake, alone."

Mrs. Benoît stared at him.

"*Impossible*," she said. "They'd be miles away by now. Your eyes — they fool you, *non*?"

"I guess so," David replied, but he did not look convinced.

Mrs. Benoît glanced at the fire and the water steaming in the pot.

"*Mon Dieu!*" she exclaimed. "Peter, *vas-y*, get me some more wood, *vite, vite!*"

I ran quickly to fetch some logs from the pile of firewood stacked outside the door. The logs were frozen and heavy and difficult to pile in my arms. As I struggled with the weight, I heard a distant shout from the gate in the palisade and looked to see who was coming.

Robert Finlay, one of the clerks on the post and a good friend of my father, was on his way to the men's house to eat. He had heard the cry as well. We both watched as a figure stumbled through the snow towards us. It was Teluah!

He was crying out, but I could not understand what he was saying. I gazed at the outflung arms and the mouth stretched wide as if something huge were trying to get out, and all I could think was, "Here's Teluah; where's Father?"

Robert looked over at me.

"Peter," he called urgently, "go and fetch Waccan, quick as you can."

And so frightened was I, that I ran off at once, carrying the logs.

I threw them down before I panted up to Waccan's door and pounded on it. Normally I kept out of his way. He was the Interpreter and highly valued by the Hudson's Bay Company, because he could speak to the Indian people in their own languages. But there were other stories, too, and Mrs. Benoît threatened her children that Waccan would come and get them if they misbehaved, so I trembled as I waited by the scarred wooden door of his small cabin.

It creaked open, and Waccan himself stood there. I could

hear children squabbling in the house.

"Please come, sir," I stammered, "Mr. Finlay needs you."

Without a word Waccan came out of his house, slamming the door behind him. I scurried back to Robert and Teluah like a small herald.

"He's coming," I gasped.

"Good," said Robert, "now away with you, back to Mrs. Benoît."

I didn't want to go but his look told me that I would not be allowed to linger. I trailed off with many glances over my shoulder, wishing that I could hear the conversation now going on between Teluah and Waccan.

"So where is my wood?" demanded Mrs. Benoît.

David laughed.

"What a memory!" he jeered. "It's a wonder you remember why your fork's on its way to your mouth when you eat!"

Blushing, I mumbled an apology and turned for the door again, but at that moment it swung wide and Robert came in. He looked grave.

"Peter," he said, "bide here, laddie. I've news you must hear though I hate to be the bearer."

In the sudden silence I could hear the hiss as the fire ignited a tiny vein of resin in the wood. The mottled blue enamel jugs and plates stacked on the shelves by the window seemed to stir and swell in the flickering candlelight. Mrs. Benoît's hands stole upwards to cover her mouth.

"There's been an accident," Robert went on. "There's no easy way to tell you. Peter, your father went through the ice. I'm afraid he's gone."

I stared dully at him while Mrs. Benoît cried out and rushed at me, pulling me into her arms as she sat down and rocked to and fro, weeping over my head. Her own children looked on astonished until their faces crumpled in sympathy and they buried them in her skirts, bawling loudly.

As for me, I was dry-eyed. I listened as Robert explained that the sled had hit a patch of weak ice which had given way under the back of the train where my father stood. Down he had gone instantly. Teluah had managed to hurl himself clear as the sled reared up, though not without a wetting. He had desperately tried to save the dogs which were dragged helplessly back into the hole by the weight. But the ice was cracking under his feet and he could not get close enough to slash at the harnesses and free them. Of my father there was no sign.

After that, Teluah's first task had been to make a fire and dry off or he would have perished from the cold, and there would have been nobody left to tell the tale. Then he had painfully made his way back to his village on foot through the snow.

The voices droned on and the babies cried, and all I could think of was the ice parting and my poor Vixen dropping silent as a stone into the black water beneath.

Mrs. Benoît's arms tightened around me and, as if from

a great distance, I heard her say, "*Pauvre p'tit.* All alone in the world. What will become of you now, *hein*?"

The same thought must have occurred to much more important people than Mrs. Benoît. Even the remote and exalted Gentlemen of the Hudson's Bay Company must have had to consider my fate. I knew nothing about that, of course, for nobody consulted me about anything, but I did overhear a conversation Robert had with the Chief Trader some days later.

I was sitting under the window of the tradestore staring aimlessly at the ice-covered lake stretching for miles to the horizon between the rounded hills. Spruce trees laden with snow marched down to the shore in battalions as far as the eye could see. At first I was not interested in the voices behind and above me. Then my attention was suddenly snared.

"We're not here to run an orphanage," snapped the Trader's voice, "this is a fur business. How am I to explain the expense of wetnursing the brat?"

"Well sir," said Robert cautiously, "who else is to do it?"

"There must be relatives somewhere. Let them take the responsibility!"

"But that's just the problem," Robert's voice continued patiently, "there *is* no family. Mackenzie told me he left Scotland when he found himself alone in the world and all I know of his wife is that she was Cree."

"He had no business taking a wife. He knew that was

against Company policy. And for good reason, as you see!"

"The boy canna be blamed for existing, sir," protested Robert. "And ye canna deny his father died in the service of the Company. The least they can do is feed the child."

"Try telling that to their Worships," grumbled the Trader. "They don't like spending the profits without any return."

"If they will just support him," said Robert, "I will see to him until he's grown and able to fend for himself."

"Well," said the Trader, "if you like hopeless causes . . . I'll tell you, I can't see that boy ever amounting to anything. A sicklier looking creature I never saw. You need stiffer backbone to survive up here as you well know. Mackenzie was a good man and he didn't make it."

"Nonetheless," Robert said firmly, "he deserves the chance."

So it was that I came under the reluctant wing of the Gentlemen in far away London, an unwelcome charge on the Company. The change in my circumstances was marked only by the removal of my little cot into a corner of Robert's room — a change for the better as he had a small fireplace like a gaping black mouth and the glow was a welcome presence in the dark — and more attention from Mrs. Benoît, who seemed to include me automatically among her own brood when it came to food and occasionally washing behind my ears.

Years later I saw the entry in the Fort's journal for 1822 which marked this watershed in my life. "Mackenzie lost thro ice," it reads baldly, "w. train and six dogs. P. Mackenzie: charge to Co. henceforth."

That says nothing of the void that opened in me like the black hole in the ice beneath my father's sled. I was not quite seven years old, alone in the world, and something of a burden as everyone kept reminding me. I was buried, hundreds of miles from civilization behind the great barrier of the Rocky Mountains, in a fur trade post perched at the end of Stuart Lake, right in the middle of the vast, empty space at the edge of the world called New Caledonia.

Nobody expected anything of me and I drifted from day to day expecting little of anybody else and trying hard to make myself invisible. No doubt I simply accepted things the way they were, and got on with the only life I knew. What more could happen to me? The worst seemed to have overtaken me already and no future event could possibly match it.

But that was before my eighth birthday. On that day in 1823, I met two murderers face to face.

❧

THREE

Murder at Fort George

"There's something wrong here," Robert Finlay muttered. He brought the packhorse to a halt and stood, studying the open gates in the palisade and the silent grey buildings beyond.

A small group of Carrier people huddled together just outside the gates. As the horses stopped, the Carrier broke off their conversation and stared silently at us. Then, without a word or sign, they turned and scattered, vanishing like wraiths into the wall of black spruce trees that pressed against the fence on all sides.

I heard the tension in Robert's voice and looked up anxiously. I hoped the trip would not be spoiled. Normally, Robert would have left me behind at Fort St. James when he was sent on one of the dozens of journeys Hudson's Bay Company employees made every year in New Caledonia, taking supplies from post to post in the vast fur trading area west of the Rockies.

On this occasion, though, Robert had given in when I had pleaded to go with him. Usually I was left with Mrs. Benoît, who kept me busy making sure her children did not fall into the fire and coaxed a smile out of me with little pats and hugs when I fell silent holding the clay pipe my father had left on the mantel the day he disappeared, so I had been surprised when Robert agreed to take me to Fort George. The fact that Benoît's wife was about to have yet another baby probably had something to do with it, but just as I was trying to think of a really good argument, Robert gave one of his rare smiles and said, "Why not? The weather's good, so there'll be no problem, and you're old enough, I reckon. Have to start sometime. Besides, it can be a birthday treat for you. But no whining, mind."

So there I was, on my eighth birthday, proud that I had handled the long trip without complaint, slowly pressing south east through endless trees on narrow trails, covering fourteen miles on a good day before stopping each night to sleep on the ground with the horses tethered nearby, their teeth crunching whatever grass they could find and their breath snorting softly every now and then, the familiar, comfortable smells of woodsmoke and the dried fish we were carrying to Fort George on the air. But now, it seemed, all was not well.

"It's too quiet," said Robert softly. I glanced at Benoît who was holding the bridle of the lead horse. Benoît looked puzzled, too, and his dark eyes flicked restlessly to and fro.

"Where's Mr. Yale?" he asked. "Surely he saw us coming?"

I knew that Mr. Yale was the Clerk in charge of Fort George. Robert and other employees regularly carried supplies to the smaller fort which stood by the Fraser River near the place where the Nechako joined it. Mr. Yale should certainly have been expecting us.

A flicker of movement caught our attention. Robert's frown deepened as he watched an Indian scurry through the gateway carrying a plump bag that leaked a thin trail of black powder as he passed us, ducking his head as he ran.

"Hey!" Robert shouted. The man ignored him and ran faster.

"Now how did he get hold of that?" Robert said thoughtfully. He clicked at the horses to get them moving again and we passed the heavy gate. Inside the palisade some very small log buildings huddled round a patch of thin grass. The only thing I could see moving was a robin scuffling through some dead leaves by the fence. Apart from that rustling, it was so quiet that I stifled my own breathing, sure that the sound would mask whatever it was that we were listening for so intently. Robert handed me the reins.

"Stay here, Peter," he said. "Benoît and I will see what's going on."

I watched Robert and the middleman march off to the nearest building, which looked as if it might be a store or warehouse, and disappear inside. I could hear Robert's harsh voice calling for Mr. Yale. A dog sidled near me, sniffing at the packs, and I picked up a stone and chased it off. I felt very small, standing in the exposed area between the weathered log buildings.

Robert and Benoît reappeared.

"Hello there!" shouted Robert, looking around the compound. "Mr. Yale, sir! Anybody here?"

There was no reply. A sudden breath of wind sent little dust devils whirling across the dusty space in front of the cabins and the horses stirred restively, jerking my arm up as they tossed their heads.

"Drat the man," said Robert peevishly. "Surely he hasn't left the post without permission? In any case, where are the men?"

Robert sent Benoît to search the tiny men's house. The middleman soon hurried back.

"*Personne*," he reported, "nobody. But if they've gone, they take nothing. Boots and such things *partout*, dishes on the table, *curieux, non*?"

"We'll look in the outbuildings," said Robert. "You start at the far side, Benoît, and we'll work toward you. I don't like this," and he laid a hand on my shoulder and steered me to the building standing on stilts directly behind the store.

Warning me to wait by the steps, Robert quietly climbed and pushed open the door. The dark inside swallowed him up. It seemed to be a cache for dried fish; I recognized the smoky smell. I could hear Robert's boots on the floorboards overhead, moving about. The space under the little building was tiger-striped with shadows, but nothing stirred among the kegs and boxes and the old dugout canoe stored there.

Once again, out of the corner of my eye, I caught a flicker of movement. There, inside the woodshed. So there were people here after all!

"Robert," I called, "I see them!"

I ran to the woodshed and plunged inside. Instantly, the gloom blinded me. Before my eyes could adjust, something clutched the front of my jacket and a grip like iron tightened about my throat. Far off I felt buttons giving way. My feet suddenly left the ground as my unseen assailant hauled me upwards, and the blood started pounding in my head as my own weight helped to choke me. I gasped in the acrid stench of sweat and smoke and fear. I saw the gleam of an eye and some teeth very close, black hair shiny with bear grease, and over a shoulder, a dreadful picture in a shaft of dusty sunlight from a small high window.

An axe had bitten into the chopping block, dark stains on its blade. Sprawled beside it lay the shadowy forms of two men. One had an arm flung across his face; the little finger dangled madly down the back of the hand by a flap of skin.

All this I saw in a searing flash. At the same moment, above the banging of the blood in my head, I heard my own name in the far distance — "Peter! Peter!" — and a strange voice much closer in the gloom. It seemed to come from below my dangling feet, and through a strangling red haze I could see that my attacker's lips had not moved. There was someone else there!

"Tzoelhnolle!" it hissed warningly.

My attacker's grip slackened. The next minute I was reeling against a wall, my hand grazing painfully against the bark chinking between the logs, and a sharp crack on my head addling my wits even further.

The man called Tzoelhnolle stared at me, compelling me to stare back like a weasel with a rabbit, then silently, slowly, drew a finger across his own throat and smiled wolfishly. His companion tugged at his arm and the two melted into the shadows. Flies buzzed noisily as Robert's tall black shape blocked the light in the doorway.

It took Robert only a second to size up the situation. He hurriedly snatched me up.

"Come away, laddie," he said. "This is no place for you."

I pressed my face against Robert's scratchy wool coat and squeezed my eyes shut, yet still I saw the smile that was no smile, and the stealthy finger sliding across the brown throat. All by itself, my body started to shake.

Alerted by the shouting, Benoît hurried up to us.

"You find them, *hein*?" he asked.

"Oh aye, we have that," replied Robert grimly. "It's murder we've got here."

How could Benoît be so casual?

"Didn't you see the Indians?" I cried.

"What Indians?" asked Robert sharply.

"The Indians in the woodshed!"

Benoît shook his head in bewilderment.

"No Indian came by me," he said.

"Nor me," said Robert. "Are you telling me, laddie, there were live Indians in there? Sure you're not imagining things?"

"No, no," I protested, desperate to convince them that they were letting the villains escape. "There were two. The one called Tzoelhnolle grabbed me, he lifted me up by my coat and squeezed my throat and I couldn't breathe and it was all dark and then your voice and the other one stopped him, I know he wanted to kill me, he threw me down and he pretended to cut his throat, but it was my throat he wanted to cut, I know it was and he'll come and get me, I know he will. Look, if you don't believe me, look at my coat."

And I showed them where the buttons had been wrenched out of the cloth and the buttonholes torn. Robert sucked in his breath as he looked at the damage. Benoît noticed something else.

"*Mon Dieu*," he exclaimed, pointing to my throat, "some-one thought you were a chicken for the pot!"

He and Robert exchanged looks over my head.

"Probably long gone by now," said Robert. "They'll make

themselves scarce. We won't see them again."

I knew Robert was really talking to me although he was looking at Benoît. Then he rumpled my hair and pressed me to his side.

"Well," he said, "I doubt you'll forget this birthday. It's not given to every eight-year-old to meet a pair of murder-ers!"

FOUR

◎

Clearing Up

A quick search of the woodshed convinced Robert and Benoît that the murderers had somehow managed to escape from a side opening without anyone seeing them. As it was late in the day, there seemed little point in trying to track them down, so the two men decided to secure the Fort once again.

They shut and barred the gate in the palisade, unloaded the supplies and fed and watered the horses. It was comforting to do something ordinary like dipping water out of a barrel into a bucket so that the horses could drink. Their smell, and the way their haunches shone in the candlelight and the deliberate crunch, crunch as they ate the hay I found for them was very soothing. But once that was done,

Robert and Benoît still had to deal with the corpses.

First, they carried the bodies into the men's house, laid them out on the big table in the kitchen and covered them with fur blankets they took off the narrow cots. Grave-digging would have to wait for daylight, but in the meantime it was important to protect the bodies from animals.

"Saints preserve us!" exclaimed Robert as the candlelight flickered on one smeared, shuttered face. "Isn't this Deyepay?"

I must have looked puzzled. Robert glanced at me and explained.

"Mr. Yale's assistant," he said shortly. "Bit of a trouble-maker."

Benoît peered and pushed some of the matted hair aside.

"*Ma foi*," he breathed, "it is. I recognize that little scar, *voici*, by the corner of the eye."

Together the two men looked at the other corpse.

"I don't know him," said Robert, "but he must be a Company man. Perhaps he's new."

Benoît nodded slowly.

"Bad thing," he said, "when *la Compagnie*, she cannot protect, not even here, at a Fort."

"At least there's a stout door here," Robert observed, slamming it shut as we left the bodies to themselves. He tugged at the latch to make sure it had caught. Benoît hurriedly crossed himself.

That done, they set up camp inside the tradestore. Benoît

discovered small caches of powder and shot under loose floorboards. Robert thought that the Indians were probably anxious about the murders and had put the ammunition in easy reach while they had the opportunity. I thought of the man we had seen scuttling away with the leaking pouch when we arrived. While Robert closed up the wooden kegs and restored some order, Benoît took an axe to the woodshed, with much crossing of himself, and fetched firewood for the tiny grate in the tradestore office.

Soon I was sitting beside a cheerful fire, eating some dried fish just as I did at every meal. It was so normal it was almost possible to forget Tzoelhnolle and his companion although they could have been anywhere in the darkness that now pressed about the tiny log buildings of the Fort. It was even possible, with Robert's and Benoît's voices rumbling peaceably over my head as they passed the rum back and forth, for me to imagine we were the only people in the whole world.

Almost, but not quite, for when we wrapped ourselves in our fur robes and lay down close to the hearth, I stared into the glowing heart of the fire and shivered as I remembered the two occupants of the men's house in their silent, chilly sleep. Only three men lived at this little outpost and two of them were dead. Where was the third?

The last thing I heard was Robert saying drowsily, "What has become of Mr. Yale, I wonder? Will we have another to bury, do you think?"

There came a grunt from Benoît and then Robert's voice again.

"Well, we'll know who to be looking for, at least." His voice slowed, almost caressing the name. "Tzoelhnolle," he said, and then there was silence.

FIVE

Mr. Yale Returns

The next day saw us stirring early, for the morning air held a promise of frost and the fire had gone out. Benoît soon blew the embers into life and I made myself useful fetching water from the barrel by the men's house and helping to prepare the fish for breakfast.

Later, while Robert and Benoît discussed where to bury the two Company servants and the problem of getting news of the murders to Officers of the Company, I gathered up my courage and ventured out into the compound.

The dark spruce trees crowded about the Fort. I could have sworn they were a little closer than they had been the day before, as if they had secretly edged forward in the night. Their vast numbers made the little clearing with its weathered log buildings huddled together like musk oxen in a defensive square within the palisade seem puny and pitiable. The only sounds I could hear were the harsh call of one of the big black and white woodpeckers with the startling red crests, and the distant thrum of the wind swelling to a roar as the gusts swept through the tops of the watchful trees, barely stirring the branches. I could see the ceaseless glide of Simon Fraser's river glinting in the gaps between the logs in the palisade. I shivered. For the first time, I felt like an intruder in this landscape. It seemed so alien and hostile all at once, so closed off and secretive. Who knew what it concealed?

As I was thinking these dark and unfamiliar thoughts, I was startled by a sudden thudding on the gate and an angry voice.

"Deyepay!" it yelled. "Where the devil are you? Deyepay! Open the gate, man!"

I ran to the tradestore to call Robert, then trailed behind with Benoît as Robert hurried to the gate and threw it open to admit a small red-faced man leading a horse. The bad temper evident in his voice seemed to have made him swell dangerously; I watched anxiously for him to explode.

"Who the devil are you, sir?" the little man demanded. "And where's that scoundrel, Deyepay?"

"Mr. Yale, I presume, sir?" said Robert calmly.

His cool tone deflated Mr. Yale a little, and he gave Robert all his attention.

"Yes," he said, "and you?"

"I, sir, am Robert Finlay. And this is Benoît. I believe you were expecting us with the supplies?"

Mr. Yale looked past him to where I stood. "And who are you, boy?"

Under his unfriendly gaze, my tongue stuck in my throat. Robert pulled me closer to his reassuring bulk.

"This is Peter Mackenzie. You may remember his father, drowned a year or so back."

"Yes, yes," said Mr. Yale, impatiently. Now that he had docketed me in his mind, I was obviously of no further interest. "I knew you were coming. I thought I'd be back before you arrived, but my horse went lame and I made no distance at all these last two days."

It was on the tip of my tongue to ask where Mr. Yale had been since he had obviously not informed anyone of his absence, and I knew from Robert's comments the night before that Officers of the Company had to get permission to leave their posts. I noticed that Robert did not ask the obvious question, however, so I stifled my curiosity, too.

"Deyepay helped you unload, didn't he?" Mr. Yale went on. "I left him in charge. And LeBlanc as well. Where are they?"

And then Mr. Yale looked around, puzzled, as if noticing for the first time the unusual silence of the Fort.

"They are lying in the men's house," Robert said. "Dead."

Mr. Yale's wandering gaze snapped back to him, the

colour draining from his face. He finally spoke, his voice wavering.

"Dead?"

"Murdered."

The Clerk's eyes bored into Robert's. "H-how?" he stuttered. "Who?"

"Two Indians," Robert replied, "one called Tzoelhnolle and . . ."

"Tzoelhnolle! I warned him! I told him to keep his mouth shut! I told Deyepay he was playing with fire over that woman! But the fool wouldn't listen!"

I could make little of this, but Robert and Benoît exchanged looks.

"A heavy price to pay for a sweetheart," sighed Robert.

"Indeed," said Mr. Yale hotly. "Imbecile! Why couldn't he listen to me?"

The Clerk was on the verge of exploding again, but Robert tactfully distracted him by suggesting that he and Benoît should busy themselves with the graves. Mr. Yale agreed. While they were digging, he said he would go in and write a letter for them to take back to Fort St. James to inform the Gentlemen of the Company about the murders.

"It should never have happened," he raged, "*would never* have happened if I had been here!"

Again, Robert and Benoît stayed silent.

I was left to entertain myself while the graves were dug outside the palisade. I played at building a fort, making pretend buildings from bark and a palisade of broken twigs. From time to time I caught glimpses of Mr. Yale, head on hand at his desk in the tradestore office, chewing the end of his quill pen, or scribbling furiously.

Eventually, just as I was constructing a flagpole of a long twig with a dead leaf skewered on it, Robert came through the gate looking hot and smacking at the dust on his trousers. He called Mr. Yale, who emerged with a shabby black book in his hands, and made me brush off my hands and knees. The three of us walked silently to the spot where Benoît stood leaning on the long handle of a spade by mounds of fresh earth. With the three men I stood by the raw-looking graves, looking down at the shapes wrapped in fur blankets while Mr. Yale read the Lord's Prayer and words about sparks flying upwards and dust and ashes. I thought about my father, and how different it had been for him, and wondered if he had minded not having a funeral, even one as rough and ready as this. When Robert nudged me and I took a handful of sandy gravel and sprinkled it on the bodies, I felt for a moment as if I were really burying my father at last and that I knew where he was, and then I was led away, while Benoît stood ready to shovel the dirt back into the holes.

That night we camped in the empty men's house, despite Benoît's mutterings about dead men's beds and my own dislike of the big table in the kitchen, even though it had been freshly scrubbed. The lamp in the tradestore was still shining when we settled to sleep; Mr. Yale seemed to be having trouble with his letter.

I was puzzled.

"Robert," I said to the bulky shape lying next to me in the attic darkness, "why was Mr. Yale so angry? Deyepay didn't get murdered on purpose, did he?"

Robert Finlay chuckled. "No, laddie," he answered. "Yon gentleman was having a wee struggle with a guilty conscience, I'd say. Going away like that when he knew trouble was brewing, leaving those jealous monkeys to their own devices, why, that was throwing fat on the fire. And telling nobody he was off! He's in the wrong of it and knows it, I reckon. Whatever comes of it, he'll be to blame."

I thought it a novel idea that guilt could look like rage. When I felt guilty, for disobeying Robert or breaking something, I always wanted to hide or make myself as small as possible, not draw attention by an outburst of temper. Perhaps this was one of the differences between children and grown-ups, I decided.

When we left the next morning, collecting the letter and saying goodbye to the Clerk, I studied Mr. Yale. The Clerk was now pale and hollow-eyed; his voice no longer boomed and his ink-stained fingers twisted together nervously.

"If only my horse had not gone lame," he lamented as we were leaving. "If only I had been here."

Just before the trail plunged into the forest I looked over my shoulder and waved. The lone figure still stood at the fence, watching. Then it turned and slowly closed the heavy gate, sealing itself from view within the silent wooden wall.

SIX

⌒

Doubts and Fears

The week-long journey back to Fort St. James was un-eventful. My perch in front of Benoît on his placid mare gave me a grand view of the narrow trail winding through seemingly endless dark trees. Sometimes we would follow the winding path of a river, pushing our way through willows and the crimson stems of dogwood, and I would see osprey fishing or watching the water from the tops of dead cottonwoods. There were steep hills to climb, too, and we would struggle up from one valley bottom and drop down again into another, the horses' sides heaving like bellows. At night we would camp in tiny clearings around smoky fires, or settle on the shore of a lake and hear loons cry unseen on the misty water. The weather was beautiful and I relished the gentle days rocking to the rhythm of Benoît's mare, watching the powerful haunches of Robert's horse clench and relax as it plodded ahead of us, but both Robert and Benoît were edgy and watchful as though they expected something to happen, and their nervousness was contagious. I was left to my thoughts for the most part as neither of my companions seemed inclined to talk.

I had much to think about. The memory of the two bodies sprawled in the woodshed intruded on my dreams, but it was Tzoelhnolle's face, the strength of his clutching hands, the smell of his hair and his sinister, threatening gesture that chilled me and made my stomach clench and revolt. I wished fervently that Benoît and Robert had seen the two murderers and prevented their escape so that I did not have to worry about them coming after me. Without being able to explain why I was so positive, I was sure that Tzoelhnolle at least would not rest until he had choked me into silence or cut my throat from ear to ear.

I felt ashamed of my fear yet I could not banish it. When we camped on the fourth night after a weary day of lurching over tree roots and rocky outcrops, during which my brain had feverishly created endless variations of my death at the hands of Tzoelhnolle, I must have looked dejected as I pretended to eat my dry, tasteless fish.

Robert's hand paused before it reached his mouth.

"What ails you?" he snapped. "You're not usually so shy

about food. Don't tell me you're sickening for something. I'm no doctor!"

Only a burning need to share my burden allowed me to speak, and even then I could manage no more than a few words.

"I . . . I'm . . . afraid," I mumbled, head hanging.

"Afraid? What's a big lad like you to be scared of, eh?"

I looked at Robert, willing him to understand.

"Tzoelhnolle," I whispered at last, when he showed no sign of guessing the cause of my distress.

"Tzoelhnolle?" Robert repeated. "But he's nowhere near us. He canna harm you, laddie."

"But he'll find me," I protested. "He promised he would. He didn't say it in words, but it was a promise just the same!"

Robert gave an abrupt bark of laughter before replying.

"Wisht, laddie," he said, "that's plain foolishness. Tzoelhnolle will be too busy saving his own skin to worry about you! The only thing you could give away was his name and he must realize that everybody knows it now. So why would he bother with a wee lad like you?"

Robert certainly sounded convincing and I had to be satisfied with his assurance, but I noticed that neither of my companions ever relaxed his vigilance as we journeyed north.

I had another question in my mind, too. When we camped on the sixth night, I took the plunge.

"Robert," I asked, "why was it so quiet at Fort George? Where did all the Indians go?"

I was used to the bustle at Fort St. James with the trappers, mostly Carrier Indians from the nearby village, coming and going with their furs, the women helping with the chores or preparing skins or drying fish, the children tumbling about the compound with the dogs. I could not imagine life without the constant presence of Carrier people, so Fort George, completely empty and silent, had been very disturbing.

Robert rubbed a hand over his head and removed his long-stemmed clay pipe from his mouth.

"I'm not sure you'll understand," he replied slowly. "Do you know what revenge is?"

I shook my head.

"Well," Robert continued, "it's like this. Suppose a man killed another man in another family. He might expect someone in that other family would want to punish him by killing him. That would be revenge. It's like the Bible says — 'an eye for an eye, a tooth for a tooth'. Now the Indians believe in this. It's their law. They knew as soon as it happened that two of their people killed two of the Company's people so they are afraid the Company will come after them for revenge. That's why they ran away."

"But why should that make all the ones who didn't do anything bad so afraid? Wouldn't the Company just want the bad ones?"

"Ah," said Robert, "that's how we would think, but the Carrier would take revenge on anybody connected with the bad ones, guilty or not, and they expect the Company to think the same way."

"So how does revenge stop?"

Robert shot a quick look at me and smiled.

"Aye, that's a good question and that's the problem. It could go on until there's nobody left, you see. But the Company will see to it that it doesn't come to that."

Benoit rumbled in agreement.

"Bad for trade," he chuckled, "and *la Compagnie*, she won't stand for that!"

Robert smiled grimly and nodded.

"No judges in long wigs to say what's what here," he said. "It'll be up to the Company to lay down the law, and she will, mark my words!"

A few days later we had struggled up to the plateau and reached Fort St. James. I was glad to see the familiar palisade and huddle of buildings on the shore of the lake, with the big red Hudson's Bay Company flag whipping bravely overhead at the top of the flagpole. I drank in the familiar vista of the long corridor of hills and water dotted with tiny islands, all in shades of blue and grey and indigo and violet, and felt glad to be home.

Benoît quickly disappeared on learning that his wife had given birth to a little boy while he had been gone, but the other employees were soon buzzing over the news we had brought back with us.

The Chief Trader, Mr. McDougall, looked grim as he read Mr. Yale's letter and questioned Robert. He shook his head in disbelief and glanced anxiously at me as Robert described how I had found the bodies and encountered the murderers, and glowered as he learned of Mr. Yale's absence. Soon he, too, disappeared to write letters of his own to be sent forward on the long journey to Company headquarters back east.

Everywhere I heard men wondering out loud what would come of this. One man who had been working at McLeod's Lake in 1821 had a theory.

"Stands to reason," he said darkly, spitting for emphasis, "it'll be revenge. Remember that time the canoe overturned and that Indian, what was his name? — Aze, that's it — Aze drowned? Well, the clerk from McLeod's Lake was in the canoe as well, and got a wetting himself, but they'll still be blaming him for the death, you mark my words, never mind it was years ago. They've got long memories, those rascals!"

Heads nodded solemnly in agreement.

Another man eagerly expanded the theory.

"Right you are," he agreed, "and wasn't Aze related to the man with Mackenzie when he went through the ice? Tit for tat, see?"

His companions noisily cleared their throats and punched his arms, nodding their heads at me, and he fell silent, looking embarrassed.

"Me, I know nothing about that," said Benoît. "But I do

know it won't be no good for trade."

I was surprised the next morning, therefore, to see a large group of Carrier Indians approaching the Fort along the shore from their village near the mouth of the creek. At their head marched an imposing figure wearing a headdress rather like a long-haired wig and a robe made of small skins pieced together hanging to his knees. I quickly ran to alert the Chief Trader of their approach. By the time the group of Indians had reached the tradestore, Mr. McDougall was standing in front of it, his arms folded, Robert and the other men at his back. I crept close to Robert's leg and watched.

For a while the two groups stared at each other without speaking. I wondered what was behind the round, expressionless faces. The black eyes gave no clue to their feelings. At last, the imposing leader in the wig greeted Mr. McDougall, who inclined his head gravely in response.

"Kwah," he said, "what can I do for you?"

I felt a flutter of excitement. So this was Kwah, the Great Chief!

The Chief spoke again. He seemed to have difficulty in finding the right words. Waccan, the Interpreter, stood ready to translate, for though the Chief apparently spoke some English, Mr. McDougall was certainly not fluent in Carrier. The exchange of remarks and the two-way translation was slow and ceremonial like a strange game with very elaborate rules.

"We have heard," he began, "of the deaths. This is bad news to us. Bad news."

Some of the younger men standing at Kwah's shoulder stirred at these words and looked at each other. One tossed his head and folded his arms like Mr. McDougall.

Kwah continued. "We feel your grief. We would not wish it so. No good can come of such things. I know. I have seen too much in my life."

The young man with folded arms glowered and stared distantly at the roof of the tradestore.

Mr. McDougall waited, giving Kwah no help, and soon the Chief continued.

"We regret the deaths," he said. "We bring gifts to show this. Here."

And he gestured at his followers who parted to allow two men through. They laid baskets full of glistening silver salmon at Mr. McDougall's feet.

"We regret," Kwah repeated insistently. Behind his back, a smile spread over the face of the young man.

James McDougall's stern expression did not relax. He looked at the young man, then looked at Kwah.

"Pick up your fish," he said harshly. "I cannot accept such a gift when some among you smile at what has happened!"

And he turned abruptly and led the way into the tradestore, abandoning the Indians on the doorstep. I thought Kwah looked worried as the Indians dejectedly picked up the baskets and trailed off to the gate.

Benoît looked worried too.

"*Ma foi*, that's a mistake for sure," he said. "Why go to insult them? There'll be trouble, *sans doute.*"

But the next day the Indians were back.

The whole village had come this time, men, women and children accompanied by several scrawny dogs. Again, Kwah faced James McDougall. Again he insisted on his regret. This time, I noticed, the young man of the previous day stood with his head bowed. This time there were no defiant looks or mocking smiles.

Once again the fish were meekly offered. McDougall let them lie on the ground and waited.

Kwah hesitated and then began again. It seemed that he was coming to the real point of his visit.

"There is something we would know," he said.

"Ask your question," replied McDougall.

"We would know how the Company intends to hunt. Are all my people in danger?"

James McDougall drew himself up to his full height.

"We are not Carrier," he said haughtily. "We do not punish the innocent for the guilty."

Kwah looked doubtful and his followers murmured.

"You will not take revenge on us?" he asked again.

"The Company does not punish the innocent for the guilty," McDougall repeated. "Of course, the Company would be well pleased with anyone who would help them to *find* the guilty."

Oh, I thought, so that's it. All the chief has to do is tell Mr. McDougall where the murderers are hiding and everything will be all right! But as soon as I thought this, I realized the chief's dilemma. How could he turn people who were probably his relatives over to the Company? Would I be able to betray a brother or a cousin if I had any? Could I deliver Robert or Benoît into the hands of enemies howling for their blood?

Kwah stared at McDougall and slowly nodded.

"We regret," he said once more and turned away, leaving the salmon, dull now, on the ground.

SEVEN

❧

Marking Time

The Carrier did not hand the murderers over to the Company. Instead, they all but disappeared.

For months, the Fort was unnaturally quiet and idle. Day followed day without any visits from Indian trappers with furs to break the monotony. Mr. McDougall's temper got shorter and shorter.

One day when Robert had set me to counting the twists of tobacco in stock, and I was laying the tarry, dark brown slabs in a line on the counter, Mr. McDougall burst out of his office brandishing a much-folded piece of paper which was weighed down with the broken remains of an impressive scarlet wax seal.

"Deuce take it, what good will this do?" he thundered.

"Closing down Fort George! That's cutting off our nose to spite our face!"

"Well," Robert said doubtfully, "I suppose it shows the Carrier we mean business. And look on the bright side — there'll be fewer trips with supplies."

"Balderdash!" spluttered Mr. McDougall. "There'll be no need of supplies. It's business that will go belly up. No fort, no furs. Frighten all the Indians away and we'll all be looking for new jobs. And you," he added as his glance fell on me, "will be looking for a new home."

"No, no," said Robert quickly, "not while I'm alive."

"Maybe not," Mr. McDougall relented, "but I tell you, Robert, trade is less than half what it was last year. We'll not survive at this rate."

He sagged gloomily onto a stool.

"And another thing," he continued, "where do you suppose they're sending our precious Mr. Yale, who might have prevented all this if he'd just followed the regulations?"

Robert's face fell and Mr. McDougall nodded grimly.

"Aye, that's right. We're to expect him within the month, though what he's to do I can't think. There isn't enough work for us now. Just an extra mouth to feed," he lamented, "but there, God has spoken, so what can we lesser mortals do?"

God, I knew, was John Stuart, the Chief Factor. No doubt the letter Mr. McDougall was folding up again had come straight from the great man.

The Trader looked at my neat rows of tobacco.

"Well, laddie," he said, "how much do we have on hand?"
I was ready.

"We have one unopened bale and forty seven twists of tobacco loose, sir, and one that is missing a corner. It looks as if mice have been at it."

Mr. McDougall smiled.

"It seems you can count at least," he said. "Maybe you'll be able to show Mr. Yale a thing or two, if he ever manages to get here without taking a wee holiday first."

Mr. Yale did arrive about two weeks later. He had a hang-dog look about him when Mr. McDougall was near, and I heard the men snickering behind his back. I noticed that he barked at everybody when the Trader was not around. Certainly he did nothing to dispel the air of nervousness and uncertainty that gripped the Fort.

In the circumstances, the task that occupied every waking moment for most of the men seemed urgent and vital. Orders had come to build a new Fort, complete with a stockade and bastions, further down the shore towards the little river that flowed into the lake just the other side of the spit of land that marked the northern end of our bay.

The work progressed at a snail's pace. A new store had gradually taken shape, and some smaller buildings had been moved to the new site, but nothing was finished. Above all, there was no protective fence round the new buildings, let alone anywhere for us to live, so we went on making do in our shabby, overcrowded quarters, much to Mrs. Benoît's disgust.

Nor was that the end of Mr. McDougall's anxiety. Letters came from the new Chief Factor, William Connolly, to say that he intended to make Fort St. James his winter headquarters. He needed a house suitable for his rank and his large family, to be ready for occupation when he arrived in the autumn.

We all became builders. Mr. McDougall pored over plans, trying to make sense of them so that he could give instructions to the men and organize the materials. Deloge, a big loose-jointed man with huge hands and a silly grin permanently fixed to his face, prepared the timber, squaring the logs and making the planks for the flooring. Whitman and Ettier and Roi helped, making plaster and preparing whitewash from kegs of white earth brought down from the village at Pinchi. Even I was pressed into service, collecting the square nails as they were made, helping to fetch the bark that was to cover the roof, selecting suitable stones for the chimney, breaking my nails and bruising my knuckles until my hands were permanently black and blue.

Perhaps it was Mr. McDougall's urgency that pushed Deloge too fast. Perhaps he was simply a bad builder. Whatever the reason, even I could see that the new house would never do. It leaned; the corners already bulged and gaped. It was intended to have bedrooms upstairs and a double chimney dividing the parlour and a downstairs bedroom. Certainly it was the grandest house I had ever seen. But the higher they got, the more it leaned, as if the house were staggering under its own weight and lurching side-ways, and I waited, fascinated, for the day it would finally collapse.

There were bad-tempered consultations between Mr. McDougall and the builders, gloomy surveys of the drunken house, accompanied by head-shaking, as Deloge, still grinning, set large timbers as props against the side that threatened collapse. Mr. McDougall finally flung up his hands and set them to levelling it before they went any further. It was better when they resumed but still not good, and much time had been lost.

More trouble came when they built the famous double chimney. It was painfully slow work, and risky because of the height. Because I was nimble and had no fear of heights, I was diverted from the miserable task of filling in the hole beneath the house, to carrying stones up to the builders and small containers of fresh mortar. I enjoyed scampering up the rough ladder, pretending I was climbing the rigging of a clipper from the Indies, an illusion fostered by the brisk wind off the water. Sometimes, in the grip of this game, I forgot what I was supposed to be doing, and woke to a shout from Deloge or an impatient clout if I was in range.

The chimney rose and rose. After two weeks it was done. Deloge straightened up, took a last critical look at his masterpiece silhouetted against a glorious fiery sunset, turned to Roi and cried, "Enfin! C'est fini!" flinging his arms wide in triumph and grinning hugely.

Exactly how it happened, I do not know.

At the time I was standing on the ladder peering over the edge of the roof. From my point of view, Deloge's gesture was followed immediately by an ominous sagging of the stones, a warning shout from Roi, and the disappearance of the proud jutting bulk of the chimney. A lot of it dropped straight down through the roof and I heard confused shouts below. Some of the top stones, soft mortar still attached, tumbled down, bouncing, just like boulders in a landslide. One particularly large one that I remembered lugging up crashed into the top of my ladder, sending me flying, still clinging uselessly to the top rung.

Fortunately, I landed in a heap of sand, the ladder on top of me. The impact punched all the wind out of me, so I spent the next few minutes gasping and groaning, trying vainly to drag in a single breath, while Deloge peered anxiously over the edge of the roof demanding that I speak to him.

Mr. McDougall was furious at the catastrophe. He knew that he could not possibly carry out his orders in time. Mr. Connolly would arrive and there would be no house suitable for him. There would be no new Fort with a sturdy, comforting palisade, and bastions housing little cannons for extra protection.

Instead, looking depressed, he gave orders to repair the old buildings as far as possible, so that we could weather the coming winter. To make room for Mr. Connolly, some of the men had to move from their building to ours, and sleep in the attic. They grumbled and I could not blame them. The first of our tasks was to replace the bark on the roof, for it was split and rotten, and when it rained, the water poured through. Some of the windows had to be boarded over, too, for we had no parchment to repair them. This made the tiny rooms even darker, but at least the wind and snow would stay outside.

I felt unsettled in this half-and-half world. Work went on from time to time on the new house, and whenever there was a spare minute, Mr. McDougall would set men to cutting and splitting the stout poles for the future palisade, but progress was very slow. The new store and the half-finished house and the piles of fence posts crouched on the chilly ground, waiting, just like us, for spring and new energy. And for Mr. Connolly.

☙

EIGHT

Enter Mr. Connolly

M r. Connolly burst into the Fort one day in October. Everything he did had an explosive quality, accentuated by his habit of barking in a loud, hectoring voice. He was a portly, black-haired Irishman with a red face and snapping blue eyes. His snowy white stock looked too tight about his neck, and I watched, fascinated, as the veins in his throat swelled and his buttons strained over his stomach as he roared.

He was not pleased with the housing arrangements.

"Is it pigs you think we are, that we should live in such a hovel?" he ranted while Mr. McDougall looked apologetic, but Mrs. Connolly, a silent, plump Indian lady, quietly took possession of the hovel and directed her children to bring in their belongings.

I liked the look of one of them, a girl a little older than me, and ran to help her carry an awkward box. She smiled at me, and thanked me prettily, and would have spoken further, but turned aside as soon as her mother called, "Amelia, help me with these blankets!" and left me no excuse to stay.

After allowing his temper full reign, Mr. Connolly subsided and disappeared into his house, kicking at the decrepit door and snorting.

It seemed to me that his arrival was a signal of some kind. Before, Mr. McDougall had worried constantly about the unfinished construction; after, he seemed to give up, for that year at least, all idea of moving us to the security of a new fort. Instead, we threw ourselves into preparations for the winter that was treading on our heels, and turned, like animals seeking out their well-tried burrows, to the familiar buildings inside the girdle of our decaying, tottering fence.

I helped stack the firewood, following the great ambling ox as it dragged the loads of timber to be cut up with the two-handed saws and split, and made the rounds of the animals, feeding the dogs and our two remaining horses.

The days grew short and cold and the first snow fell from a leaden sky, muffling our little world in complete silence. Somewhere in the trees, the Carrier people were huddled round the fires in their winter houses, too, but for all we knew of their whereabouts, they could have been on the far side of the chilly moon that turned the night a strange, ghastly blue.

We crowded into the kitchen of the men's house in the long evenings when the wind whined in the chimney and Robert and Benoît and the other men, and Mrs. Benoît, too, sometimes, puffed contentedly on their clay pipes and my eyes pricked with the smoke. The men played cards, and Mrs. Benoît sang, and sometimes Robert would read to me from the big volume of Shakespeare's plays which was one of the few books at the Fort apart from the Company Regulations, a book on salt water navigation, a battered Bible, an ancient atlas and a copy of Bishop Berkeley's *Theory of Vision Vindicated and Explained*, which were stacked on a shelf over the Trader's desk in the office.

I loved listening to Robert read. At first I just listened and followed his finger as it stroked the page, but soon I could make out the words for myself. Robert claimed that there was really no poet to match Robert Burns, but he allowed that Shakespeare was a close second, especially in *Macbeth*. It wasn't long before we were chilling our audience with "Glamis hath murdered sleep, and therefore Cawdor shall sleep no more, Macbeth shall sleep no more!" and Amelia and I — for she would steal in to join us sometimes, until her father came to complain of the noise and shooed her back — were dancing round the fireplace draped in fur blankets, our shadows capering huge on the wall behind us, chanting, "Double, double, toil and trouble, fire burn and cauldron bubble."

The stout logs of the cabin walls sealed us snugly from the creaking cold and blazing stars outside. Days had grown into weeks and weeks into months without a whisper of Tzoelhnolle and his companion. If you fear something horrible and nothing actually happens, it is impossible to stay frightened all the time. The Company's apparent anxiety to complete the new fortifications kept the possibility of danger alive in my mind, but the sharp edge of my terror had gradually dulled and I found whole days slipping away without a thought of the murders.

But the murderers remained at large, and nights were another matter altogether.

At this time, one dream began to invade my sleep again and again and wake me, sweating and gasping, in the dark.

With no warning or explanation I would find myself falling in pitch darkness, the smell of earth strong and bitter around me. I would flail my arms in terror, tearing my hands on stones and roots, trying to stop, my hair streaming like flames above my head, a wind roaring in my ears, and my mouth stretched in a gaping, silent O as I plummeted.

Then I would land with a fearful thump and pitch forward on my knees.

Still in the dark, I would crawl about, feeling my way, and learn that my prison had carefully squared corners and smooth sheer walls. It was a grave. A very deep grave.

Far above I would see a rectangle of light. Distant voices murmured. I would shout and scream for help, then a wavery head would float to the edge of the grave. It was Mrs. Benoît.

"What do you want, *mon p'tit*?" she asked.

"Please," I begged again, "please help me out. I'm not dead."

"Don't be silly," replied Mrs. Benoît, "of course you are. *Sois sage*, now, and don't make any more fuss."

More heads bobbed into view. I saw another I recognized.

"Robert," I howled, "I don't like it!"

Robert's head gazed back at me.

"There's something wrong here," he said. "That's no place for a lad. But there's nothing to be done. It's the law."

And all the heads would nod solemnly in agreement.

"Nothing to be done," they chorused like bells tolling, "nothing, nothing," and their faces would sag with the weight of the word, the features sliding, eyes drifting past noses, ears slithering down necks, every one melting and dwindling before my horrified gaze into pools that spilled greasily down the walls of the pit.

Now I would smell bear grease and spin round, certain of what I would see.

There was the dim shape, the gleam of the greased hair, the white of an eye, the shining teeth. The finger sawing to and fro across the throat.

The smile broadened with a swishing sound. An axe blade flashed out of the dark.

My only hope was to climb out of the pit, but to do that

I had to stay out of reach, and the walls seemed to be closing in now and stretching upwards, more like a chimney than a grave.

To the terrifying whistle as the axe flashed from all sides out of the dark, I would make my last desperate lunge upwards, scrabbling frantically at the walls.

"Go on, go on!" I would scream at myself, willing my fingernails to become claws so that I could climb as easily as a bear cub. But I was clutching nothing but air. Suspended in that last moment, my arms flung high, I saw with hideous clarity that I was lost.

Somehow all my fingers hung by the merest thread of skin and dangled in a fleshy fringe, tapping limply against the backs of my hands as I slid down and down in a bruising hail of boulders to watch, paralyzed, the final glittering swoop of the axe.

And then I would wake, rearing out of sleep into the lonely dark, my breathing loud and ragged, tears streaming down my face. So vivid was this dream that I would hold up my hands, certain that the fingers would be dangling uselessly, and strain to catch the whisper of the blade.

Sometimes Robert would wake and assure me it was nothing but a bad dream. He would settle me down again and tell me to go back to sleep, and soon he would sigh and his quiet snores would rumble once more.

But I would wait, wide-eyed, for the looming shapes in the room to assume their familiar shapes in the frail light of dawn and fight to stay awake. It was safer that way.

What I could not possibly know was that another problem loomed, so serious that it could make nonsense of all my night fears. Another eight months and we would face a terrifying spectre that could claim us all as victims, the innocent with the guilty, and threatened a summary end to my brief and inglorious career.

Starvation.

NINE

❧

Crisis

On a warm afternoon in August then, when the sun leaped sparkling from every tiny movement of the lake, and the air was ringing with the sounds of the men building the new palisade, I heard Mrs. Benoît's voice calling me from the kitchen of the men's house. I left the two little Benoîts I was minding to their noisy play with a pile of pebbles, and ran to see what she wanted.

"Oh, Peter, *mon cher*," she said as she straightened up, flushed, from hanging a large iron pot full of water to boil over the fire, "I need some more fish from the cache. I thought I had some here, *mais non*. Get me enough for tonight, *s'il te plaît*." And she handed me a large, ornate key.

I rarely had occasion to visit the cache, and paid it little attention except in the fall, when I would help to stack and hang the year's supply of dried fish inside out of the reach of animals. As long as meals appeared on the table each day, I gave it not a thought the rest of the year.

But it had been the scene of unusual activity in the last few weeks. David had been set to counting the fish in the store more than once, and I had seen Mr. McDougall and Robert emerge from it one afternoon, deep in conversation, their faces grave.

When I asked Mrs. Benoît what was happening, an anxious expression, quickly smoothed away, crossed her face.

"The stores, they are low, a little," she said. "But don't worry yourself, *mon p'tit*, the salmon will come."

She stared through the open door of the kitchen at the lake, wiping her red hands on her apron.

"They will come," she repeated slowly, but she did not sound convinced.

After that I became more alert. Portions were certainly smaller; Mrs. Benoît was doing her best to stretch what remained. The men also tried to supplement our diet. Sometimes they paddled out on the lake and returned with small kokanee or char, deliciously fresh, but not enough to satisfy. David turned out to have unexpected skills, learned, he said, from a father who had been a poacher in the Old Country. He begged a handful of barleycorns from Mrs. Benoît, soaked them in rum and lured three grouse to a drunken end. He was also very handy with wire snares, and brought home several rabbits.

Mrs. Benoît welcomed everything that could be caught, including squirrels, but we knew it was just a stopgap. If the salmon run failed, our staple, the food that we ate at every single meal, would not be available. No supplies could be sent to make up the deficiency; they came just once a year. We would starve.

Robert and Benoît had already gone to Fraser Lake to see if they could pick up a load of whitefish to tide us over. They had been gone a week. An air of desperation lay over the Fort.

Even before they left, I had heard Mrs. Benoît appealing to Mr. McDougall.

"What am I to do?" she had asked. "These men, they cannot eat the air!"

Mr. McDougall had looked harried and smeared a hand across his face as if to clear away cobwebs.

"Robert," he had said, "send a couple of men up to Pinchi to pick berries. They can be there and back in a couple of days. That's better than nothing, I suppose. No rest for the wicked," he grumbled, turning back to his books. "If it's not one thing it's another. Just do the best you can," he added to Mrs. Benoît, who was still hovering in the doorway. "We'll all have to tighten our belts a wee bit."

The Carrier had been busy repairing their great horn-shaped fish traps with spruce roots for weeks at their village just down the curve of the shore from the Fort, where the river spilled out of the lake. Men had been down at the river every day, gazing into the water, willing the silver backs to appear, and scanning the air and trees for signs of the eagles and ospreys that would prey on the salmon and the crows that hung around for the carcasses once the fish had spawned.

I had sensed the dread that hung over us, but nobody would tell me exactly how much food was left or how long it would last. Now was my chance to find out.

I ran across the compound to the fish cache, a section of the warehouse partitioned off from the furs and goods. I slid the key into the lock. It was stiff and I had to struggle with both hands before I heard the click as the key turned and the door, parched and furrowed from the sun, and warm under my fingers, swung open.

The interior was cool and shockingly dark after the sunshine. Even so, I would have known where I was if I had been led there blindfolded.

The timbers breathed fish. In my mind's eye, I visualized the year's supply hanging from the stout rafters, and piled on the floor, thousands upon thousands of gutted, opened, flattened, dessicated corpses, all a curious shiny orange as if they had been shellacked, their spines clearly visible like decorative beading on varnished wood. I had once seen an atlas which showed strange maps of the world, quite unlike the charts I was used to. They looked as if a globe had been cut open from north to south, and then slashed at the poles so that the sphere could be opened out and laid flat. The result was a map with curved petals along the top and bottom, pieces of land or oceans split apart, and whole countries bent and leaning sideways in a most unnatural way. These dried boards, their fishy features in unexpected places, reminded me irresistibly of those maps and their odd view of the world.

It was a shock when my eyes gradually adjusted to the dim light. The beams of the building and the fish were almost the same warm colour, so I did not immediately realize what I was seeing.

When I did, my hand flew to my mouth and my breathing tightened. My eyes flicked from one fish to another, counting silently. One, two, three, four, five. My count slowed. Eight. Nine. Ten. Ten. There were just ten fish in the store.

I went further into the cache, searching the shadows at the back. I disturbed a bat, but found no more fish.

Ten fish. Eight people. Four fish a day each.

It was late in the year. Not a single fish had arrived. We were going to run out of food tomorrow. Starvation suddenly loomed.

Hurriedly, I took down five of the fish, shut the door of the cache and ran back to Mrs. Benoît.

"I've brought you five," I panted. "That's half. There are only five left."

Mrs. Benoît stared at me.

"Ssh, *tais-toi*," she said warningly. "No need to tell every-body the bad news. They'll know soon enough." She took the five rigid fish from me. "Go and make yourself useful, now."

Unenthusiastically, I wandered out to the garden. The prospect of weeding made me feel exhausted, but I picked up a hoe much too long for me, and toiled up and down the rows of potatoes and turnips, hacking listlessly. I noticed that the potato leaves were limp; had there been a frost last night? Could we lose that crop too? Mr. McDougall was right. There was always something to go wrong.

When I had finished, I went on to my special job, which I usually enjoyed, but the food shortage cast its shadow even here.

It was my responsibility to feed the sled dogs, and har-ness them when they were needed. There were over thirty dogs at the Fort, large animals with coarse, dense grey and white fur. The dogs were invaluable. They could work ef-fortlessly in deep snow. I had once seen two dogs pull a load of three hundred pounds, and they routinely covered twen-ty miles in five hours. They didn't eat as much as horses, either. Generally, they would work untiringly on the same fish we ate every day.

I loved the dogs for their enthusiasm; unlike the men, they actually relished their work. When they sensed that they were going out, their tails seemed to become even curlier, and they danced and jumped, nipping each other and howling deafeningly. They needed no urging; at the first command they were off at a dead run and woe betide the inattentive driver, for if he was caught off guard and lost his grip on the harness or sled, he would lie helpless in the snow while the train disappeared rapidly into the distance!

In the winter, I was very careful not to allow any dog to run free and tire itself out in this way. The person who allowed that to happen got an automatic beating.

I loved to watch them settle down to sleep, winding themselves until they were coiled tightly, then wrapping their plumy tails over their paws and noses like giant mufflers.

They never looked for shelter, even choosing to sleep on the snow in the open in winter. Many times I have watched the sleeping forms gradually whiten as the snow softly fell and fell. But on those winter nights so clear and cold that it seemed the air must splinter and shiver into a million, tinkling shards, when the Northern Lights rippled and swelled across the sky, the dogs would waken and howl, filling the night with song, as if they, too, sensed the great silent chords that I could feel shuddering in my head as the lights swirled majestically overhead.

In the summer, the dogs didn't work, of course, but they still had to eat. They were tied up along the stout posts of the palisade, just far enough apart that they could not turn on each other to fight over the few scraps I was able to beg from Mrs. Benoît to give them. The big ones always bullied the smaller ones given the chance, and I was anxious to protect one undersized puppy that I regarded as my special dog.

He was the only one left of a litter the mother had hidden beneath the old store. Unfortunately, they had all fallen sick and died, including the mother, save for one. David called it the Runt, and teased me when I begged to look after it and keep it as a pet. Sometimes I think I was allowed to keep it only because everybody expected it to die immediately. But I made it a bed of old socks and laid it by the fire in the men's house, and coaxed it to lick fish pounded into a kind of wet paste with water from my fingers, and carried it about with me, and against all the odds, it thrived.

As soon as it became obvious the puppy would live, I gave him a name. He had a patch of white fur between his eyes like a star with many points so I called him Blaze.

As he grew bigger, Mrs. Benoît had refused to have him in her kitchen any more. But outside he had to join the other dogs, and so he, too, was tethered to the fence, although I often slipped him off the leash and took him with me when I scrambled about the creek and the lakeshore.

David was setting out with a fishing pole over his shoulder as I passed.

"Hey, Peter," he called, "is that dog of yours fat enough yet? If I don't catch anything, we'll be needing him for dinner!"

I ignored him, but the question made my stomach squirm. Dogs did appear on the table from time to time; in fact, we had eaten dog at Christmas as a special treat! And at times like this, when everyone was so hungry, the dogs sometimes mysteriously disappeared, despite the beating that inevitably followed if the thieves were discovered.

The dogs yipped at me excitedly as I approached. I had only a few scraps and I felt guilty, giving them so little. They had such beseeching, puzzled expressions as they snuffed about the ground where a fin or tail had fallen, and then gazed intently at me as if my face would give them a clue where it had gone. I made sure Blaze got his share but I could not bear to stay with them as I usually did.

Instead, in an effort to forget my own hunger I wandered down to the lake to watch the canoes being built.

I was drawn to them irresistibly. They reminded me of my father. I could remember him in the prow of a canoe, his paddle stabbing the water in powerful strokes, pushing it smoothly aside, making the craft glide effortlessly over the surface. Canoes had taken him far and wide; how I envied the skill that could set him free from this little place and push the horizons back!

The canoes were an act of faith, too, on the part of the Company. Although I could never have put it into words at that time, I was reassured by the optimism that assumed there would be trade next year, and people alive to strike the bargains and ship out the furs, and thus a need for new canoes.

It was a big job. The Company had decided that there were so many trips with supplies and returns now that Fort St. James was the depot for the entire region that we needed three large freight canoes. Waccan was put in charge of the project, and he had immediately set about collecting the materials, storing them in the warehouse until they could be used.

For months, he had searched the area for suitable trees, emerging from the bush with great rolls of birch bark on his back supported by a tumpline about his forehead, or lengths of fir which he then painstakingly split, or coils of spruce roots, some twenty feet long or more.

Even I had helped. One day I was sent up the hill to the north of the Fort with a small bark basket and a knife to look for wounded spruce trees, and returned with sticky fingers, a basket full of the amber resin that bled from the damaged trees and coagulated on the bark, and a clean fragrance that clung about my clothes and hair and skin and made Mrs. Benoît hug me and sniff appreciatively and say, "Oh, you smell good enough to eat, *mon p'tit!*"

At the beginning of August Waccan had chosen a flat site on the lakeshore to build the canoes and erected a makeshift shelter of saplings covered with spruce boughs to keep off the sun. Under the shelter the first canoe was half completed.

The birch bark had been soaked in the lake and unrolled, dark side up. The canoes were to be twenty-five feet long, so the bark had to be pieced together and the seams carefully pared down and sewn with spruce root, which had been split along its length and soaked to make it pliable. The sides of the bark had been turned up and supported in a frame of stakes which marked out the shape of the finished boat.

One day had been devoted to carving the long timbers for the inner and outer gunwales with the curved canoe knives and the drawknives, which were blades with two perpendicular handles that you pulled across the wood towards you. I had tried it, and discovered just how easy it was to jam the blade in the wood. The gunwales had been soaked, too, then steamed to bend them to the correct shape. There was a fire burning at all times, with big river stones heating by the flames; pouring water on the stones produced clouds of steam.

That afternoon Waccan was presiding over the ribs. The bottom of the canoe had been held down with stones to help preserve the shape, but these had been removed, and the inside of the canoe was now sheathed in wide strips of fir. Waccan's dark face, heavy with the black moustache, and shrouded by the broad brim of his hat, moved in and out of clouds of steam, bending the strips for the ribs, two at a time, turning them into squares with one open side. Then he put the lower rib in place, forcing the ends down under the gunwales and knocking the rib upright into place with taps of a mallet, moving the top rib of the two into the next position, where it fitted perfectly, being slightly narrower.

Before my eyes, all the raw materials of the canoe were falling into place, wood and root and bark magically transformed into a beautiful thing with flowing lines, the ribs curving symmetrically as the veins on a poplar leaf or the delicate bones of a fish.

The day rolled by. By late afternoon, Waccan's helpers had fitted the cap on the gunwale, fastening it with wooden pegs, and my spruce gum, carefully heated and mixed with bear grease, had been painted on to all the seams and the outside, and allowed to dry.

Waccan summoned a little group of boatmen, including Benoît, to try the canoe on the water for the first time, to test for leaks.

Carefully, they righted it, lifted it off the ground and walked with it into the shallow water. They set it down gently and it floated, buoyant as a leaf. Benoît waved at me, beckoning.

"*Vite*," he called, "you can have a ride."

I looked at Waccan to see if he would permit this. I took nothing for granted where he was concerned. He gave a barely perceptible nod, and I scurried down the slope, hobbling over the stones on the shore in my bare feet and splashing into the water. Benoît hoisted me into the canoe.

"*Voilà*," he said, "right at the bow, where your father would have been."

And I knelt at the prow, like a small figurehead, gazing down the narrow lake, the long watery corridor between the blue and purple hills that led, it seemed, to the end of the earth. I clutched the gunwales on either side, wishing that I had a paddle that I could dip into the crystal water and send this magical craft skimming over the glittering path laid down by the sun, just as my father had done so often.

Other men climbed in, because this was a canoe for five men, unmanageable with just one or two. Their weight brought the water line closer, but the canoe still felt as light as one of the twigs I sailed on the creek in the spring when run-off was at its height.

"Dry as a bone," commented one of the men as we paddled slowly along the shore, and there was an appreciative murmur. My spruce gum had done its work well!

Waccan was pacing along the shore parallel with us.

Suddenly, I saw his head lift and point, like a gun dog. I looked in the same direction and realized that there was a man running from the gate, shouting. At first, it was just a wordless cry.

"Waccan!" the man cried. "Two men. Out there." His arm flung itself toward the dark wedge of spruce trees beyond the palisade. "Skulking around in the trees. Been there a while. Trying to hide!"

Waccan flung down his canoe knife and straightened up. He beckoned us urgently and the canoe returned to shore. He gave quick instructions to the men, who scattered instantly. Moments later, they reappeared, armed with guns. As they rejoined Waccan, I heard the Interpreter speak. I heard only two words clearly, but they were enough to galvanize me.

"Murderers," I heard, and then "Tzoelhnolle!"

The name froze my blood. All my fears rushed back to fill my head to bursting. They *had* come back! What else could they have come for but me?

My first impulse was to run and hide in the darkest corner I could find, to burrow beneath a building or plunge into a great pile of furs and shut out the sight and sound of the world.

But then I gave myself a shake and told myself, as Robert frequently did, to be logical. The murderers were the ones who were pursued, not I. Besides, they would never dare come to the Fort in broad daylight, would they?

So who were these men? And how were they going to fare at the hands of Waccan, who had rushed off with the light of battle in his eye and had never been known to shrink from execution? I was the only one here who knew what Tzoelhnolle looked like. Perhaps I was the only one, too, who could prevent an overhasty miscarriage of justice. Besides, I told myself, knowing for sure whether the skulkers were the murderers or not was much more bearable than ignorance.

I was convinced.

I had to go into the forest myself.

TEN

❧

Reprieve

I crept out of the Fort behind Waccan and his little band.

I was proud of myself for staying out of sight, slipping behind bushes and moving from tree to tree keeping my eye on Waccan's broad brimmed black hat. The men ahead of me spread out as they entered the forest, stepping cautiously and frequently halting to listen and look about them.

I did the same. It was very still under the trees. I was sure that my heartbeat was loud enough to betray me. I gasped as a grouse erupted from the ground by my foot and clattered off into the shadows.

The distraction was momentary, but by the time I had

recovered, Waccan and the others were out of sight. I moved forward cautiously. I saw a glimmer of a light colour over to my left. One of the men with Waccan had been wearing a moosehide jerkin. I turned toward it as it flickered in and out of the dappled shade ahead.

It did not seem to be moving very fast, and now I could hear the low murmur of voices. That was odd, when they were trying to take the skulkers by surprise. I eased forward and peered round a massive trunk.

In front of me was a little saucer-shaped dip in the forest. Two men lay in it, both Indian.

I caught my breath, but then relaxed, for I had seen neither of them before. They were both very thin, and lay listlessly, their ribs showing clearly as they breathed.

At that moment, a twig snapped under my foot. At the instant that the Indians turned in my direction, Waccan and his companions appeared at the other side of the depression, their guns levelled. Waccan barked a command as the Indians scrambled to their hands and knees and the heads swivelled back to him. They froze.

I leaped out from behind the tree, desperate to prevent a mistake.

"Don't!" I cried. "They're not the ones!"

In his turn Waccan started and swore. The guns jerked and wavered.

"*Pardieu!*" said Waccan. "Stupid boy! What are you doing here?"

"I wanted to see if they were the murderers. I wanted to make sure," I mumbled.

Waccan stared darkly at me, then his gaze softened and he nodded.

"So do we all," he said, "so do we all."

He turned his attention to the two Indians and spoke to them in an unfamiliar tongue. They replied at some length, though their voices sounded weary and feeble.

Waccan grunted.

"Starving," he said. "Come from Babine hoping to find some food at the Fort." He laughed mirthlessly. "I've told them they're out of luck, we're no better off. If those fish don't come soon, we'll all be finished."

The men tucked their guns under their arms and moved off, the Indians straggling behind dejectedly. I wished I had something to give them; their pleading eyes were as hard to meet as the dogs'.

Back at the Fort, I wandered aimlessly into the warehouse. I hoped I would find something there to take my mind off my growling stomach. Waccan was telling Mr. McDougall that the skulkers had not been the murderers as hoped. McDougall sighed.

"A pity," he said. "We need to get that matter cleared up. The Carrier are still staying away from us, I notice. We'll be lucky to send off a hundred bales this year."

He glanced down at his ledger and shook his head.

"It's a bad business altogether, and bad *for* business, too.

You must do what you can, Boucher, to encourage Kwah to work this winter. No more gambling!" He sighed gloomily. "If the salmon would only come! We'd all breathe easier then. No sign of them, I assume?"

Waccan silently shook his head as he left.

I hung about in the corners, keeping out of the way, hoping nobody would hear my stomach complaining loudly, until Mr. McDougall noticed me and beckoned me forward to help sort the furs. I perked up a little; I always enjoyed listening to the Trader softly keep up a running commentary on the pelts heaped under his hands.

"See that, Peter," he said, brushing a beaver pelt the wrong way so that the soft downy underfur was clearly visible. "That's what all the hats are made of, not the long hairs on top. That's what we came here for. Odd thought, isn't it? Now see this one — what's this d'you think?"

"Weasel," I replied promptly, stroking the small brown sliver.

"Just so," said McDougall, "but that's his summer jacket. Now show me his winter coat."

I rummaged through the skins until I found a white fur, tipped with black, and held it up.

"Well done," said McDougall, beaming. "Now it's called ermine and will end up on the king's cloak, perhaps."

My hand was drawn to stroke a long slender shape with short dense oily fur.

"Hands off that otter!" Mr. McDougall barked. "The

guard hairs will curl if it's handled too much."

I quickly obeyed, not wanting to be sent away, but Mr. McDougall seldom held on to his irritation and soon started talking again.

"Now see here," he said, holding three pelts draped across his arm. They were all the same shape, but one was very dark, almost black, another small and a warm brown, and the third a bit larger with an orange patch where the throat had been.

"These are all pine martens," Mr. McDougall went on. "Which do you think is worth the most, eh?"

I considered. I thought the one with the orange splash was pretty, but I remembered Robert telling me that weasels with a yellow patch were worth less than ones without. And it seemed to me that the marten without the orange throat was too small. I pointed to the very dark one.

"Very good! We'll make a trader of you yet! The darker, the better, with martens. Like sable, d'you see."

I had heard of the legendary black sables of Russia. Mr. McDougall chuckled as he pulled out an odd fur, striped black and white, and shaggy.

"You know what some rascals do with these?"

"But that's a skunk," I said. "Who'd want that?"

"There's many a fine skunk had his white stripes dyed, been given a good haircut, and passed off as a Russian sable!"

I smiled at the image of a skunk having a haircut. Mr.

McDougall handed me an armful of pale, creamy furs so soft I wanted to bury my face in them.

"Hang them up for me," he said.

I carried the lynx pelts behind the big fur press. Balancing on a stool beside the beaver skins stacked like glossy pancakes on the floor, I hung the pelts beside their brothers, tenderly stroking the dense fur and setting the dangling legs with their heavy paws swinging slowly in the shadows.

Mr. McDougall snapped his ledger shut. For a moment he stood musing, then his quiet voice broke the peaceful silence.

"This is the heart of things, here, laddie. Without the furs, without all these little deaths, there is nothing."

The quiet words filled my head. I could feel them slide in and lodge fast. I looked about at the hanging furs, at the massive, shaggy bearskins and the narrow fishers who had once preyed on porcupines and the plumy fox tails like clubs made of feathers and the swaying silvery lynx, and saw the chanciness of life, even the animals mere forfeits in a game they did not even know they played.

The next day dawned grimly enough. David groaned weakly as he rolled unwillingly from his bed in the corner of the kitchen and climbed into his trousers. I snorted as they slid about his ankles again when he slowly reached for his suspenders.

"Every morning," he complained, "I'm in more and more

danger of slipping through my breeks altogether and falling into my boots!"

He could joke, but everybody was thin, and moved listlessly about their tasks. Mrs. Benoît clucked over her children; their eyes seemed to have grown much larger and their skin was almost transparent. I had caught a glimpse of myself that morning in the sliver of mirror that Robert had tacked to the wall in our room to help him shave, and a similar ghost with dark shadows under its eyes had stared back.

But my sombre mood did not last long. As I lugged more firewood to the kitchen for Mrs. Benoît, another figure ran shouting through the gates.

It was a Carrier, bursting with news.

"*Talo! Talo!* Salmon!" he cried.

The Fort leaped instantly into life. All of us dropped whatever we were doing and rushed to the river bank. I passed Mrs. Benoît scurrying along with a ladle in one hand and a small child in her arms. The canoe makers still held their crooked knives as they raced along the shore. Even Mr. McDougall joined the throng in his waistcoat and shirtsleeves, a quill pen tucked hastily behind an ear.

At the river we found a crowd of excited Carrier men, some holding the huge basketwork fish traps, others with dark nets made of the bark of mountain alder boiled black in its own juice to make the fibres invisible in the water. Yet others were in canoes, helping to manoeuvre the traps and nets into position.

All eyes were on the river. At first I could see nothing but then a fish jumped clear of the water and, as if that were a signal, the sinuous forms pushing against the river's flow became apparent. There were dozens, no, hundreds! In fact the river seemed to have curdled somehow and was thick with fish.

Some of the salmon betrayed the suffering of their long journey from the sea. They were blotched with white peeling patches like mildew blooms, their fins ragged and torn. Others were already turning red. Crows jostled each other in the trees, cawing excitedly.

There was a shout from Chief Kwah, who seemed to be directing operations, and the first trap slid into the water. It was the beginning of a frenzy. The next few days passed in a blur of writhing silver bodies and orange flesh as the fish were scooped out of the water, gutted and opened out by the women, and spitted to dry or smoke. I staggered under poles laden with fish and collected the offal to feed my dogs. The entire world was made of fish; for a time it was all we could see and feel and smell. Fish scales glistened all over us, and the air was filled with alder smoke and the joyful cries of bird and man alike as they fell on the returning salmon in a passion of relief and gratitude.

By the end of September, the fish cache held thousands of dried fish once again, the spectre of famine banished for another year.

I was as relieved as anybody, but I was left with an odd sense of dissatisfaction. I could not believe that lurching from fear to boredom to catastrophe was all that life was about. Something was missing. I looked about me at the other people of the Fort, hoping that they would provide a clue. They were all familiar and friendly; I loved Robert and the Benoîts, big and little; I could talk to the men and Mr. McDougall and Amelia; even Waccan's silent sons would occasionally allow me to tag along when they went fishing. But there was nobody, I suddenly realised, of my own age, not a single person who could be expected to share the same interests and enthusiasms, and be a companion.

More than anything else, I saw, I longed for a friend.

ELEVEN

❧

A Dangerous Encounter

My wishes were met in a way I could never have imagined.

Another winter had ambled past, and I was restless. My own body seemed to share this need for movement; I had shot up an inch or so, although I was still very small for my age, and suddenly there was a lot of wrist and ankle showing at the ends of sleeves and trouser legs. In addition, it was a beautiful day, one of those flawless days of late spring or early summer when the sun stood high in a hard blue sky. The air was full of the scent of balsam, and tender leaves of the freshest green opened like new butterflies on the cottonwood trees. It was far too nice to stay cooped up at the Fort; I had asked if I could go to the creek and fish there.

I held my breath while Robert decided. He would never have allowed me to go out on the lake on my own, for it could be dangerous, whipping itself in minutes to an angry grey flecked with boiling whitecaps when the squalls poured down the long narrow waterway. But the creek, spilling into the lake just behind the little headland to the north-west of the Fort, was harmless enough even with the spring run-off, and even if I caught nothing, its rocky course and sun-spangled shallows were endlessly fascinating.

"I don't see why not," Robert said slowly. I was already turning to go, when Robert stopped me.

"Not so fast!" he said. "Watch out for bears; you don't want to meet one now, when they're so hungry. Benoît said he'd seen a big one on the shore just yesterday. Just make plenty of noise; that'll scare them away."

"I will, sir," I said, inching toward the door of the warehouse.

"And if you see a cub," Robert called after me, "get away from it!"

"I will," I promised as I pushed the door open.

"And be back here by suppertime!"

I was already out of earshot.

Soon, Blaze and I, rod over my shoulder, were beyond the palisade and trotting through the forest. It was dark and very cool under the trees. In the hollows where the sun never reached there were still patches of snow. The bare trunks of the trees stood straight and close all around, and the silence was absolute. I found it easy to imagine wolves following me unseen, slipping quietly from tree to tree, biding their time. I hurried as fast as I could, whistling softly to myself, just to hear a noise.

As I neared the creek, the spruce trees gave way to tall poplars and cottonwoods, and I found it difficult to move quickly through the tangle of underbrush and willows. Blaze found it much easier to squirm through the tangle and disappeared from view. There was a trail of sorts, a narrow flattening of twigs and grass which seemed to be going in the right direction. I followed it. At one point I came across a fallen spruce tree, some of its roots waving high in the air, a cavernous hole beneath the ones still in the ground. There was a strong smell of fox near the hole and I thought I knew what had formed the path I was following.

A few minutes more and I could hear the creek. The water was chuckling over its gravel bed. I passed a small clearing filled like a bowl with sunlight and could see the glint of water through the willows ahead when I heard something close behind me.

It was a crunching, snapping, rustling sound, as if something heavy were blundering through the bush. Oddly, it seemed to be coming from several different places, but as I strained to hear, my attention gradually fixed on the clearing I had passed but could still see.

All of a sudden, a round black mass rolled out of the bushes on the far side of the clearing. The ball came to a halt in the middle of the patch of sunlight and broke apart into two separate shapes. It was a pair of bear cubs!

I watched, entranced, as the little bears wrestled together and chased each other round the clearing. They pretended to fight, nipping at each other, swatting the air with their clumsy paws and rolling over and over.

So engaging were the cubs that I almost forgot Robert's warning. All at once I realized my peril. Where there were cubs, there was bound to be a mother bear, much larger and fiercely protective! Where was she?

Even as I cautiously looked about, I became aware that I could once again hear the blundering sounds in the bushes. This time, though, it was something much larger moving between me and the creek. It was coming nearer. I was caught between it and the cubs!

The hair on the back of my neck bristled and I was finding it difficult to get enough breath. Suddenly, a grey shape hurtled out of the bushes and raced towards me, its tail between its legs. It was Blaze. As if in slow motion, I watched helplessly as a massive black shape pushed the willows aside and followed him onto the path.

It was the mother bear! In his terror, Blaze was leading her straight to me!

I was close enough to hear her rough breath and the little grunt of alarm as she caught sight of me, or smelt me, and stopped dead in her tracks.

I risked a glance over my shoulder. Blaze had disappeared again. I hoped that the cubs had run into hiding, but they were still in the middle of the clearing, watching with interest. If I ran away from the mother, I would be going straight towards her cubs. She would think that I was threatening them!

I looked nervously back at the mother bear. I could see her tiny eyes fixed intently on me. It seemed silly to talk to the animal, but there was not much else to do; soothingly, I said, "It's all right, nice bear, nice bear, I'm going now," and took a small step back along the path.

The bear made a hostile coughing noise and reared up on its hind legs. My heart banged in fear. I had no chance against this monster! I could see its teeth gleaming and the bright pink tongue, and the huge curved claws on its dangling forepaws.

I knew I had no way of escape except the path. The brush on every side would hamper my flight; struggling through it would be like stepping into snares and leg-hold traps. The trail was my only chance of moving quickly.

Suddenly I remembered the foxhole under the fallen spruce. If only I could reach that before the bear reached me, I might, just might, have a chance.

And it was now or never. As I half-turned to make sure the way was clear behind me, I heard the bear's angry snorting grow louder and sensed rather than saw that she was dropping to the ground in order to charge.

Without wasting another second, I wailed in terror and ran. Branches slashed at my face, roots reached out and tripped me, but I scrambled on, hands held out in front to part leaves and twigs, breath tearing in my chest, half weeping, half sobbing. Behind me there were cracks and splintering noises, galloping footfalls gaining relentlessly on me.

But there, just ten feet away, was the foxhole!

I hurled myself towards it with the last of my strength. But just as I was throwing myself down to squirm under the roots, I felt the dead weight of the bear's paw strike my leg. My own momentum pulled the paw down my leg and I felt the searing pain as one claw hooked into my calf and tore a fiery trail to my ankle before ripping free.

Instinctively, I burrowed deep into the ground. The hole was not big, but it curved underneath and between the tree roots. By folding myself smaller than I ever believed possible I was able to squash into a tiny cave, and lay there, my heart hammering and my legs clutched tightly against my chest.

There was nowhere else to go. Would it be enough?

As if to answer, the bear snorted loudly at the entrance to the hole. I could hear it padding about the tree. For a moment I thought that it had given up and was going away, but there it was again, at the entrance. I could smell its rank smell. And now I saw a paw stretching down the hole toward me, heard the claws rasping on the soil, raking at stones. The bear was digging me out!

I scrunched farther back against the earth wall. The bear was tearing at the fallen tree now, wrenching off great splinters and sheets of bark. There were little landslides of dry earth and small stones from around the roots; more and more tiny spots of light leaked into my refuge.

I found myself moaning softly, saying "No, no," as if that might stop the bear. But the claws came nearer and it was obvious that at any moment they would spear me again and drag me out. I could no longer think at all. Blindly, I lashed out with my feet, kicking and struggling, and shouting, "Go away! Go away! Leave me alone!" as loudly as I could, determined that at least the bear would not get me without a battle.

All at once I realized that I was kicking the air. I stopped shouting and lay still. The bear's bulk no longer filled the entrance to the hole. And there was a voice, saying something I did not understand.

TWELVE

✑

Cadunda

"*Sus! Sus! Nailgwúlh!*"

The voice was high and commanding. By twisting in the hole and peering up, I was just able to see a pair of bare feet and a few inches of leg. They looked rather like my own, except that the skin was a warm brown instead of fish belly pale.

"*Hani!*" the voice went on. "*Sus! Nailgwúlh!*"

Now I was certainly not fluent in Carrier but it was impossible to live at the Fort, rubbing shoulders with the Indian trappers and their families, without picking up at least a few words for common things. I seemed to have a knack for languages, too, for Mrs. Benoît had been surprised at how quickly I had absorbed French phrases and often spoke to me in her native tongue without bothering to translate.

I recognized the word for bear — *sus* — and realized that the person outside was actually addressing the animal, telling it to listen and go home. Who was this person who talked to bears as if they would obey? Didn't he understand he was putting himself in danger?

The voice fell silent and there was a maddening interval in which I could make out faint rustling noises. Then, just as I thought I could endure the suspense no longer, a face, upside down, appeared in the entrance to the hole.

"*Sulh' útanelh k'us 'et tandálh?*" the face asked. "Are you coming with me or staying?"

I needed no further invitation. I struggled to uncurl my cramped limbs, pulling myself round by the tree roots that had helped to defend me, so that I could crawl out. My clawed leg was very painful and all but useless, and I needed the strong grasp of my rescuer's hand to heave myself out of my prison.

Once upright I smeared a trembling hand across my face to erase the shameful tears and looked at the person who had conversations with bears.

The boy — for it was a boy — was exactly my height. His black hair, threaded with a few porcupine quills stained red behind one ear, hung long and straight either side of a round smooth face. Apart from a pair of hide leggings he wore nothing. He looked down at my leg which had started to bleed again with the activity and drew in his breath sharply as if he shared the same pain.

"*Soo 'a,*" he said. "Hurry up!" and he took my arm and put it round his shoulders.

"Where are we going?" I asked. I summoned up my limited store of Carrier words. "*Nts'e?*"

"To my village," the boy answered in English. "It is closer."

" I don't even know your name," I said.

"I am called Cadunda," said the boy. "My great uncle is the chief."

"But you know English," I said in amazement. "How?"

Cadunda smiled. "Last winter," he explained, "we found a white man lying in the snow on our trapline. He had a broken leg. We cared for him. My uncle told me to learn to talk to him, so I did."

"Why?"

"My uncle is a wise man. He says it is good for one of us to know what your people say even though Waccan tells us."

I was impressed by this reasoning. "Perhaps I should learn more Carrier," I said.

Supported by Cadunda, I managed to hobble away from the fallen spruce. Soon, we were on a track that I had missed completely when I came, and before long we were in sight of a huddle of tents made of skins, smoke from fires rising lazily above them. It was the summer village of the

Carrier people on the lakeshore. Beyond it I could see the flagpole of the Fort with its red flag, and the solid grey shape of the warehouse roof.

Cadunda hurried me towards one tent which had a large wooden rack outside. A beaver pelt was stretched tight by thongs across the frame and a young woman carrying a box of some sort on her back was scraping at it with a serrated bone tool. Cadunda called quickly to her in Carrier.

"Mother! This boy is hurt. A bear nearly caught him."

Cadunda's mother looked at me and then at my leg. Her head was cocked on one side and her eyes were shrewd and bright, rather like a knowing little bird. Even her movements were abrupt and unexpected, but her touch, when she investigated the wound, was gentle. She launched into a torrent of words, none of which I could follow, but I felt that I was in good hands and relaxed.

A little girl came running. She looked at my leg, grimaced in sympathy, and darted off.

"My sister," said Cadunda. "She is fetching medicine from my grandmother."

I wondered in some alarm what form this medicine would take. I had seen men at the Fort slapping bear grease on cuts, or taking what Robert called Painkiller from little brown bottles for every ill, from stomach ache to compound fractures. These measures never seemed to be much good, although the Painkiller certainly made the sufferers forget their misery for a while. With no doctors anywhere in New Caledonia, however, the little brown bottles were the only hope, and sometimes they were not enough.

I wasn't sure that what I had seen of Carrier medicine was much better. Once, I had watched a shaman, a medicine man, perform his magic over a sick child at the Fort, one of Waccan's daughters. This started with the shaman being given presents. Then the shaman had sung a melancholy song, joined by several of the patient's family, and performed a mysterious ritual, with strange gestures and the casting of swansdown into the air. This, Robert explained, was to persuade the bad spirits that had caused the sickness to leave the sufferer. The child had died, though, and the shaman had to return all the presents.

Cadunda's sister was soon back, carefully carrying a container made of pin cherry bark. Cadunda's mother dipped a piece of moss in the liquid it held and washed the long claw mark on my leg. The wound was ragged and an angry red, but the bathing soothed it.

"That feels much better," I said shyly. Cadunda translated and his mother smiled.

"My grandmother boils spruce bark for the medicine," said Cadunda. "Everyone goes to her when they cut themselves."

Next Cadunda's mother mixed some spruce gum and bear grease together, spread it on the wound, then bound sphagnum moss in place on my leg with narrow strips of hide. She smiled at me and spoke quickly. I looked inquiringly at my interpreter.

"My mother says it is good to get it clean. Bears have dirty claws," Cadunda explained.

I summoned up my limited Carrier.

"*Musi*," I said. "Thank you."

Cadunda's mother smiled again and set her daughter to clearing up while she returned to the skin she had been working on.

I stood up, feeling awkward.

"I have to go," I said.

Cadunda nodded. I said goodbye to Cadunda's mother and sister, and the two of us slowly made our way out of the village, past the hide tents and the racks of gutted fish drying in the sun, past a man mending a hole in a net with a little wooden tool and another crouched by his fire using a river stone to chip tiny flakes from the edge of a smaller stone he was fashioning into a point for a fishing spear, away from the smells of wood smoke and spruce boughs and animal skins. As we followed the curve of the lakeshore toward the Fort, I ventured to ask some more questions.

"Cadunda," I asked, "how did you get the bear to go away?"

"I told it to go home," said Cadunda. "I told it to look after its cubs."

"But weren't you afraid?"

"Why should I be afraid? The bear is my helpful spirit. It will not harm me."

"How do you know the bear is your helpful spirit? I don't understand."

"When I was old enough, I fasted and went alone into the forest. After three days I was lost. The bear came to me in a dream and showed me the path. He saved me then. Why would he harm me now?"

I was mystified. I did not understand what Cadunda was talking about, but I had seen the result and was impressed. My new friend was so sure of his belief that I, remembering my own terror as the bear tried to dig me out of the hole, was humbled.

There was something else I had to find out.

"Cadunda, why does your mother carry that little box?"

"Oh," said Cadunda airily, "that's my father."

At my blank stare, he laughed and continued.

"It is our custom," he explained. "My father died last summer. My mother will carry the ashes from his funeral fire for a year or so."

I could think of nothing to say to this.

When we arrived at the Fort, Robert was in a fine state. Blaze had returned hours before, and knowing how inseparable we were, Robert had been anxious. He showed it as anger, but when he saw the state of my leg and learned the whole story, he, too, was grateful and impressed. He thanked Cadunda for saving me and insisted that the boy take his own small penknife as a gift.

Later, Cadunda and I faced each other at the gate of the Fort. I did not quite know how to say goodbye. I wanted to see Cadunda again but I had no idea if the boy felt the same about me. There were no clues on Cadunda's smooth round face.

"I was going fishing when I met the bear," I said hesitantly. "Do you like to fish?"

Cadunda smiled.

"If you go fishing," he said, "you'd better let me know. Obviously you need looking after, just like my little sister!"

I cried out in protest and aimed a mock blow at Cadunda's head. Cadunda giggled and ducked. I went on, sure of my ground now.

"Do you want to go tomorrow? We could meet on the lakeshore, halfway between here and your village."

Cadunda nodded. "If the sun shines," he said. "We'll meet when the sun is overhead."

I nodded and watched as Cadunda turned away. The small figure soon melted into the dark trees and I was alone. I was happy, though, despite my throbbing leg, because I felt quite certain that my loneliness was at an end.

❡

THIRTEEN

Exit the Second Murderer

The summer of 1826 was a happy time for me. Cadunda was a constant and lively companion; together we swam in the lake and tickled basking trout in the creeks, searched for wild strawberries and ranged the forest and shore, looking for signs of those animals whose fur was so important to the Company.

I learned to identify the marks made on trees by big bears, and the flattened circular places in long grass where they slept. Cadunda took me to a place on the south side of the lake where bald eagles nested year after year at the very top of a huge cottonwood. We regularly visited the tree to wait for a glimpse of the eagle chick on the enormous untidy platform of branches, demanding food from the parent birds who would sail in with fish in their talons, then perch on the rim of the nest, tearing off morsels and stuffing them carefully into the infant's mouth.

We were always on the alert for the tell-tale signs of beaver — the trees not quite chewed through all round their base, balancing nervously on finely chiselled points, and saplings felled haphazardly, dragging in the current of the creek. Often we heard the slap of beavers' tails on the water, and sometimes saw their blunt noses creating bow waves as they swam to and fro across their ponds. I knew that Cadunda would be noting where they were. Beaver pelts, after all, were the most important furs to the trappers.

I was a frequent visitor at the Carrier summer camp. Cadunda's mother and sister always welcomed me, and gradually other Indians got used to seeing me there, and some would call out *"Hadih"* in greeting as I passed.

Cadunda and I went berry picking, and later we helped spread out the huckleberries and saskatoons and wild raspberries to dry in the sun, or mashed them so they could dry in flat cakes for the winter. Cadunda's mother would store them in her collection of bark baskets or woven grass bags.

Cadunda's mother would always feed me, so I enjoyed whatever she had on hand — tidbits of salmon cheek and fish roe, sweet crisp ribbons of pine cut in the spring from just under the bark, slices of waterlily root. Out in the woods with Cadunda, I nibbled like a mouse at the outer rind of the scarlet hips on the wild roses that filled the air with such sweet perfume in June, and peeled and ate the long hollow stems of cow parsnip, unless we had a fancy to turn them into flutes, instead.

When we could borrow a canoe and cross the lake by the small island just above the place where the water narrowed and poured into the Stuart river, we would paddle up to the swamp on the other side and watch the great blue herons pacing cautiously through the reeds, stabbing with their long beaks and working the hapless fish round to slide headfirst down their throats. We tried our hand at imitating the ducks that swam busily through the rushes in the winding waterways of the swamp, but the only result was a panicky clatter of wings as the birds all took off in fright.

On one occasion, and in spite of dire warnings from Robert, we climbed the rocky cliff at the base of the mountain the Indians called Nakal Dzulh that rears up from the north side of the lake. Our target was the nest of a peregrine falcon that Cadunda's sharp eyes had spotted as it dropped from the cliff face.

We did, in fact, get close enough to see the downy white chicks on that windy ledge, but at that moment, the parent bird returned screaming, talons out, almost beating at our heads with its wings. One fearful glance at the cruel open beak and fierce eye and I ducked instinctively, squeezing my eyes tight shut. Immediately, I lost my grip and slid helplessly in a rattle of small rocks and gravel, leaving plenty of my skin on the rock face as I dropped.

A dead tree which had once poked its way to the sun through a cleft in the rock and eked out a miserable existence all alone for a few years saved me. A broken branch, hard as iron, speared my pants as I slithered past. Abruptly, I was suspended in space, hardly daring to breathe. There were other branches to cling to, and after experimenting with two that snapped in my grasp, I found one that seemed reasonably secure and managed to relieve some of the strain on my torn trousers.

Cadunda eventually clambered down to me. He found a toehold for one foot, which made me feel safer, then helped me to unhook myself from the miraculous branch and climb down the rest of the way.

Neither Robert nor Mrs. Benoît, when she saw the state of my clothes, was very pleased with me. My expeditions with Cadunda came to an abrupt halt for a while, and Robert made it painfully clear that I should make myself useful and attend to my education. He wanted me to enter the employ of the Hudson's Bay Company, at Mr. McDougall's suggestion, and he was determined that I would be a credit to him and a useful servant to the Company when the time came.

I could already read and write fluently, and knew my times tables backwards and forwards. Robert even showed me how to keep simple accounts and balance debits and credits, something only the Clerks at the Fort could do. I found it easy, and was proud to earn Robert's praise for my neat penmanship and accurate arithmetic.

"You'll be an apprentice in no time!" Robert commented approvingly. Even Mr. McDougall seemed impressed when he peered shortsightedly over my shoulder at the ledger I was working on.

I felt very grown up and clever when Benoît or Mrs. Benoît listened admiringly to my reading, or when Waccan's children crowded about me, demanding that I write out their names so they could see what they looked like, marvelling that I could do so easily what they found so difficult even to copy.

There was one respect, though, in which I still felt very small and vulnerable. The murderers continued to roam at large, and Tzoelhnolle's face still tainted my dreams. I would wake, sweating, in the small hours and struggle with a dreadful sense of menace, but I said nothing, for I was sure Robert would laugh at my fears and tell me I was too old for such fancies.

But events conspired to prevent me from forgetting. Although it seemed at times as though Fort St. James were the only place in the world, so remote was it from anything that could be called a town, let alone a city, it was in fact the hub of the vast area called New Caledonia. Freight came in and went out constantly. The furs collected at Fort Fraser and McLeod Lake and Bear Lake and all the other tiny forts and outposts throughout the year eventually found their way to Fort St. James where they were pressed into bales and shipped out again, down the Fraser past Fort George and Alexandria, on to Fort Okanagan and then way down to Fort Vancouver on the Columbia River to start their long sea voyage to Europe.

With the freight and the furs inevitably came information. Packers and visiting Company Servants or Officers brought news and instructions and gossip and rumour, and poured them all into the starved ears at the Fort. Later, they would carry away answers and requests, corrections, additions and embroideries and set them adrift in the wide world beyond the palisade like so many paper boats caught helplessly in the current of the stream.

Many of the rumours had proved to be groundless, but now much more definite information arrived in the early autumn with a packer bringing leather from the Rocky Mountains.

The packer was a morose, unfriendly man given to brooding silences in a cloud of smoke from his pipe. Nevertheless, when he took his pipe from his mouth, surveyed its bowl glumly, and said, "You heard the news, I reckon," he had a ready audience in the kitchen of the men's house.

Everyone waited, but the packer sucked maddeningly at his pipe until Robert demanded, "Well, spit it out, man!"

"It's a lesson," the packer said mysteriously. "Be sure your sins will find you out! We all come to judgement in the end."

"To be sure," said Robert, as the men stirred impatiently

round the fire, "fine sentiments, no doubt. But what the devil are you talking about, man?"

"Why, that villain from Fort George, of course. Gone to meet his Maker, hasn't he?"

My attention sharpened.

"Which one?" I asked. "Tzoelhnolle?"

"Nope."

"Tell us exactly what happened," commanded Robert. "Why do we have to drag it out of you?"

The packer removed the pipe from his mouth.

"Well," he drawled, "as I heard tell, this other villain was with family, just a few of 'em, camping out near the headwaters of the Smoky, not so far from Tête Jaune Cache. Now I don't know the ins and outs, but they say this wild bunch of Cree come out of the hills and set about the Carrier for some reason, if they needed a reason. Murdered the lot," he finished with a dreadful relish, "women and children, too."

I shuddered. I could not feel very sorry for the Second Murderer, even though the man had prevented Tzoelhnolle from harming me, but I pitied the other members of that little family, who had no guilt except by the accident of birth. What kind of justice was it that attacked the innocent? If this was God's judgement, I did not think much of God as a judge. I kept this to myself, though, because the others in the audience seemed happy enough at the outcome, and were still hanging on the packer's every word.

"They do say," he went on, "that murdering rascal's body was burnt, too, partly, at least. Now why would they do that, d'you reckon? Who would have put that idea in their heads, eh?"

"You're not suggesting the Cree were carrying out some-one's orders, are you?" asked Robert incredulously.

The packer wagged his finger and looked knowing. "Them as knows can tell," he said. "Them as knows, nam-ing no names and telling no lies. That's all I can say."

"Well, that's not much and little to the point," Robert rejoined tartly. "But I suppose we must thank you for the information. Perhaps now it won't be too long before the other villain is laid by the heels and we can all sleep at night. Tomorrow wouldn't be soon enough for me."

Me too, I thought, looking round the group of men. I was startled to see that they were all nodding and murmur-ing in agreement. Obviously I was not the only one who harboured secret anxieties!

The word spread quickly. The next day, when I met Cadunda, my friend looked grave. Cadunda wasted no time in coming to the reason for his unusual seriousness.

"The bodies were thrown on the fire and eaten by dogs, they say," Cadunda began. "Is that true?"

I tried to play down the more lurid rumours. Cadunda looked unconvinced and went on with his real fear.

"It was the Company taking revenge, wasn't it? They must. A death must pay for a death, everyone knows that.

But," he continued, "whose death? Will any Carrier do? Even the innocent?"

In my head, I heard the packer saying, "Them as knows can tell," and imagined the bodies of women and children lying by the ashes in the hills. The Company couldn't have done that, could it?

"They wouldn't do that," I said, to reassure myself as much as Cadunda. "Mr. McDougall said so, when the murders happened. He said the Company only punishes the guilty. Ask your great uncle Kwah. He asked the same question."

"But how can we believe that? There has to be revenge. I could be the next one to be punished. And what do you think my great uncle would do then?"

I stared at Cadunda. My friend's words opened up a horrible vista of attack and counterattack. The worst of it was that Cadunda and I would be on opposite sides. That was unthinkable. Frightened, I clung obstinately to the promise I had to trust.

"The Company won't hunt the innocent," I insisted. "They've said so, over and over. Why don't you people just give the guilty one up to the Company and have done?"

Cadunda looked at me.

"Would you give up your cousin to *us* when we asked, even if he had done great wrong?"

I had no answer.

"Well," I said awkwardly, "we'll just have to hope it works

out somehow without getting us in a mess."

Cadunda nodded in agreement and we both tried to put the matter aside by going to help Robert and the men unload and sort the leather outfit that the packer had brought. We were busy enough hauling the dressed skins, the parchment, thirty pounds of sinews and two thousand fathoms of pack cord out of the sun into the dim reaches of the warehouse. There the dust motes dancing in the single beam of sunlight through the open door, and the furs dangling from the rafters, and the heaped blankets glowing dully against the weathered timbers of the walls as we clattered up and down the stairs were comfortingly ordinary, but the disquieting thoughts of revenge and loyalty would not go away. I did not feel at all sure that events would not affect us. In my experience, the affairs of adults almost always spilled over onto me in some unpleasant way, and I felt quite powerless to stop it.

FOURTEEN

ↂ

Cadunda Makes An Enemy

O n a fine day in the spring of 1827 Cadunda came to
the Fort with some furs. I met him at the gate and
Cadunda proudly showed me the results of his own trap-
ping under his uncle's guidance.

He had seven weasels, a lustrous mink and two beaver
pelts. I could see that the furs were of fine quality; the
beaver, in particular, were large and quite unmarked. Mr.
Connolly, who was just getting ready to set out on his usual
summer inspection of all the outposts, would be pleased.

It was important to keep Mr. Connolly happy. He was a
volcano of a man. His uncertain temper rumbled constantly, flaring into volleys of loud curses at the slightest provo-

cation. More disturbingly, some of his eruptions would be accompanied by blows with whatever came to hand: belts, axe handles, chunks of firewood, skillets, or failing a convenient weapon, his own hard fists.

Benoît called this Irishness. "He's very Irish, today, that Connolly," he would whisper in warning after witnessing yet another outburst.

Robert Finlay had another name for it. "Club law," he said. "The only thing some of these rascals understand."

Mr. Connolly certainly had some difficult men to control. In fact the thought of his employees frequently set off his rages.

"Refuse!" he shouted at his new Clerk, James Douglas. "Scum of the earth! When are they going to stop sending me the sweepings of all the gaols in Christendom?"

I knew which man the Trader was raging about. The workers at the Fort changed constantly. Nobody volunteered to live there; everyone knew that life was harder there than anywhere else. Men came and went, not always staying long enough to receive their yearly wages. The Company had to take whomever they could get. Gaston was one of these transients. He had just turned up one day, hitching a ride with a supply train. He had black hair that grew low on his forehead and a luxuriant beard and side whiskers. Two narrow dark eyes, a snub nose and a mouth that twisted in a permanent sneer crowded together inside the ring of hair. He was silent about his former life, but talked incessantly in a prodding, needling way, making jokes that stung, and complaining. Ever since he had arrived, he had been trouble. He set friend against friend, he had secretly killed a dog for a private feast, he pestered the women, stole from the men and abused the Indians who came to the Fort.

I knew that Gaston and his like were the real targets of Mr. Connolly's anger. Still, I tried to stay out of his way as much as possible although I noticed that the Factor's family did not seem unduly afraid of him, especially his pretty daughter, Amelia, which made me wonder if Mr. Connolly's bark wasn't a good deal worse than his bite.

"Come on," I said to Cadunda, "let's go to the tradestore. I know Mr. Connolly is there. He'll buy your furs, and then you can get something from the store for yourself, if you want."

Cadunda looked reflective. "Perhaps there will be enough made beaver to buy a white blanket," he said. "My mother would make me a fine capot from that to wear when I go hunting in the winter."

The made beaver was the Hudson's Bay Company's own currency for paying the trappers. One made beaver was a token that stood for the cash value of a good beaver pelt, and that was the standard for judging what any fur was worth. Cadunda would have to show the trader his furs, then the trader would offer him, say, two made beaver for the lot. If he accepted, he would get two porcupine quills to take to the store and exchange for whatever goods he wanted up to that value. Two made beaver would certainly buy him the blanket he had his eye on.

We turned to cross the compound but before we got to the store, a figure slid round the corner of the men's house and cut us off. It was Gaston. He was grinning.

"So, what you got there, *copains*? Furs? Show me."

I stepped between the outstretched hand and Cadunda.

"We're taking them to Mr. Connolly," I said firmly.

"Mr. Connolly, is it? What you want to do that for, *hein*? I can save you some time. Mr. Connolly, he don't want to be bothered with *les enfants. Vas-y!*" And he shoved me aside and snatched the furs.

We watched helplessly as the big calloused hands ran through the furs, pitching them contemptuously to the ground. Out of the corner of my eye, I caught a flash of blue. A quick glance showed me Amelia carrying a basket of washing, but she had her back to me and was hurrying away. No help there. Gaston continued his sport.

"*Mon Dieu!*" he said mockingly. "You call those furs? Mr. Connolly, he will laugh in your face!"

Cadunda bent to pick up his pelts, but Gaston's foot stamped on his hand.

"*Ecoute*," he said, leaning heavily and ignoring Cadunda's attempts to free himself, "I'll do you a favour. I'll take them off your hands. That's fair, *n'est-ce pas*? *Alors*, what you say?"

A final shift of his weight made Cadunda cry out, then Gaston lifted his foot, and as Cadunda snatched his crushed hand away from the heavy boot, and nursed it, rocking silently, Gaston swept up the furs.

"I'll take that as *oui*," he said. "*Et voilà* — a fair price."

On the ground in front of Cadunda he threw a pair of fish tails, dry with age, the kind of rubbish given to the dogs, which even they rejected. Once again, he smiled.

"Come again, *p'tit sauvage*," he said.

His smile was abruptly erased by a roar behind him. Mr. Connolly, despite his bulk, had somehow managed to creep up unobserved. Amelia was behind him, her round face pale and concerned. Her father erupted.

"Stop that, you godless hooligan! Mary, Michael and Joseph, give me strength! Take that, you worthless scum, take that and that!"

He punctuated his tirade with blows from the harness he held in his hand, quite unconcerned about where the lashes were landing as Gaston tried to protect himself.

"Steal, would you, steal from a child! Damnation and hellfire for you, boyo!"

Cadunda and I stood motionless. In the space of a few seconds our tormentor had become a cowering victim. Nor was his humiliation over yet.

"Pick up those furs!" Mr. Connolly roared. "And give them back to their rightful owner!"

On his knees, Gaston scrabbled in the dust for the pelts.

With a cry of impatience, Mr. Connolly snatched them from him and beat them against Gaston's head to loosen the dirt, just as I had seen Mrs. Benoît do when cleaning mats against the walls of the cabins.

Mr. Connolly handed the furs to Cadunda and bowed.

"My apologies, sir," he said.

He turned back to Gaston and his voice rose again. His toe nudged the fish tails lying on the ground.

"Fair payment, is it? Well, my lad, what's sauce for the goose is sauce for the gander. There's your supper. And I hope you relish it!"

With that, Connolly picked up the stiff tails and rammed them into Gaston's protesting mouth. By this time, a number of men had come to watch the show, and the sight of Gaston on the receiving end for once, spitting out fish tails, his face screwed up in disgust, made them snigger appreciatively.

I noticed that Mr. Douglas had taken the opportunity to stand close to Amelia and was whispering something to her that was making her blush. But more importantly, when Mr. Connolly ushered Cadunda into the tradestore and up to the counter as if he were a valued customer, personally handing over the porcupine quills and entering the transaction in the ledger, I saw the naked hatred on Gaston's face. The incident might be over as far as the Trader was concerned, but not for Gaston, and I shivered with a thrill of fear for my friend.

༄

FIFTEEN

A Winter of Discontent

Cadunda stayed away from the Fort after that. As the frosts deepened and the days grew shorter, the Carrier people packed up their summer camp by the river and moved off to their winter houses, long log buildings in the woods close to a good source of fuel for the fires that would burn constantly for the next few months, the smoke rising through an opening in the roof.

My life turned inwards too. There was little traffic between posts once the fish had been stored, the wood cut and the year's returns packed and hauled away. The Fort settled into its dreamy winter state, the grey buildings huddled in the snow on their little eminence above the frozen lake, smoke from the tiny chimneys standing straight up in the still air, the inhabitants concentrating on keeping warm and whiling away the empty hours.

Mr. McDougall was gravely ill. He lay in his narrow bed, as he had for weeks, motionless. Most of the time he faced the wall of rough, square-cut logs as if he were making a close study of the moss and mud chinking, except that the light from the tiny parchment-covered window was much too dim for him to see anything, even from that close. Nobody knew what was wrong with him, but his condition was obviously serious.

I was sent to Mr. McDougall's room with the meals Mrs. Benoît prepared for him. I tiptoed in, carefully balancing the tray. Sometimes Mr. McDougall would be asleep and I would stare at the blue eyelids in the wasted face and hardly dare to breathe. Usually, though, the eyes were open and followed me as I moved about the tiny room.

"Your dinner, sir," I would say and there would come a faint murmur from the bed.

"Set it down, lad," Mr. McDougall would say. "I will get to it later."

I tried to encourage him to eat, even offering to help him, for I knew that the Clerk was unable to turn over in bed and his left hand and arm were uselessly feeble. But he had no appetite and I could sympathize. There was nothing appealing about dried fish even when you were healthy.

One day, when I laid the tray at Mr. McDougall's bedside, a thin hand gestured at me. I bent nearer to the sick man. The hand clutched my sleeve.

"You're a good boy, Peter," said Mr. McDougall. "Kind."

The effort of speech seemed to exhaust him and his eyes closed. I thought I had better go and tried gently to detach my arm from his grip. The eyes opened again.

"Fetch the box on the dresser for me, laddie," whispered the ghostly voice.

I looked at the only other piece of furniture in the room apart from the bed. It was a chest of drawers. On the top, arranged with military precision, were a pair of tarnished silver-backed brushes, a shaving mug and a badger hair shaving brush, a tiny miniature of a lady painted on ivory and framed in silver, and a small box of inlaid wood.

There was nothing else. I realized that I was looking at the earthly possessions of Mr. McDougall. The man had nothing else in the world. I felt sure that Mr. McDougall was going to die; it seemed terrible to come to the end of a life with so little to show for it. I bent to look closely at the miniature.

"My mother," sighed the voice from the bed.

The tiny portrait showed a delicate figure in a curled white wig and an elaborate gown of green silk.

"She's very beautiful," I said.

"Ay, she was bonny. And a fine lady. Gone, even before I left home."

The sick man sounded very sad. His tone reminded me of a question I had long had in my mind.

"Mr. McDougall, sir," I asked, "why is it that so many of

the Company's servants come from Scotland?"

Mr. McDougall sighed. "Need drove us away, laddie. We left a hungry land." He laughed, a little rustly sound like two brittle twigs rubbing together. "Trust the Scots to pick a land like this to make their fortunes. Now, laddie, the box."

I picked up the box and carried it to the bed.

Mr. McDougall awkwardly opened the lid with his right hand. His fingers slowly sifted the contents and closed around something hidden under the papers.

"I want you to have this," he said. "I've been watching you. You'll go far. You'll find it useful. It's served me well since my father gave it to me when I first left Scotland, but I'll have no use for it now."

He put the object into my hand. It was a handsome steel-cased fob watch which lay comfortably in my palm like a cool egg. Overwhelmed, I flicked the catch on the side and opened the little cover to reveal the face. It was a clear, bright white with delicate Roman numerals and ornate hands like arrows.

Mr. McDougall appeared to enjoy my speechless pleasure and surprise.

"Look after it," he said. "I will like to think of you using it."

I found my voice and started to thank Mr. McDougall, but the sick man held up his frail hand to stop me.

"Put the box back now," he said. "No need for thanks. I

think I'll sleep a wee bit," and he closed his eyes.

I returned the box to the chest of drawers and after a last look at Mr. McDougall, quietly left the room.

I saw little of the Clerk after that. With the uncanny talent he had already demonstrated for appearing when he was needed most, Cadunda appeared one day at the gates, on snowshoes, muffled in the white blanket that his mother had transformed into a hooded cape. He was carrying a small birchbark packet.

"For the sick man, your friend," he explained as he opened the packet to show me the contents. Inside were pieces of dried bark and some shrivelled berries. I sniffed at the berries. Juniper.

"Cook, in water," Cadunda continued. "Drink. Good medicine here," and he thumped his chest.

"How do you know this?" I asked. "Did your grandmother send it?"

"She teaches me what she knows," he replied. "I will need it soon. I am to be *dayun-un* one day — medicine man — and I will drive out bad spirits and cure sickness."

He spoke proudly, but then his expression changed.

"And if I don't like you, I will *make* you sick, too!" he added mischievously. "That Gaston better watch out!"

He slipped away again and I handed his gift to Mrs. Benoît who looked after Mr. McDougall, mostly. I don't know if the medicine was responsible, or even if Mrs. Benoît gave it to him, but the sick man did survive the winter and as soon as it was possible, was shipped out to return to the east in the hope that he might recover fully.

I felt I had lost a friend, one who had some interest in what was to become of me, and Robert certainly missed his fellow Scot. For Mr. Connolly, though, it meant a serious gap in his staff. He turned more and more to young Mr. Douglas to fill the hole. As a result, James Douglas was a frequent visitor at the Officers' house that winter. Mrs. Connolly, a Cree lady like my mother, indulged him, and Amelia seized every opportunity to talk with him, coming to the store with little gifts of food she had prepared or moccasins she had beaded just for him.

Having James Douglas as an ally could not ward off trouble for Mr. Connolly, however. I listened to the talk around the fire in the men's house and in the corners of the warehouse, and knew that all was not well.

Even Benoît grumbled, especially after his wife produced yet another baby to add to the four they already had.

"How they think a man keeps a family?" he complained. "Work like a dog for next to nothing." His accent grew stronger with his distress. I knew that his older children often had to stay indoors because they had no shoes to wear outside, and regularly wore handed-down clothes that became progressively more ragged with each wearer.

Gaston could often be heard encouraging those who felt they were underpaid.

"You don't see *les Officiers* go without, or waiting for

their money after they slave *depuis une année*," he said as the smoke from his pipe drifted up to the low ceiling, and the other men, who rarely agreed with him, nodded their heads.

"I'd like to see some of them high and mighty mucka-mucks last a year here," growled another middleman, "and then be happy with nineteen pounds!"

But at that moment the latch rattled and Waccan poked his head in at the door, turning his dark gaze on them briefly as he looked for somebody, and the men fell silent.

But their discontent was not stifled. Even Mr. Connolly realized that it was not fair to expect men to work in Fort St. James without some extra hardship money. I listened to him dictating a letter to Robert in the tradestore office one day, objecting to the practice of paying the same wages in the north as in the comfortable south, "although," he bellowed angrily, thumping his desk, "the labour and mode of living between the two will bear no comparison!"

Mr. Connolly's face was, of course, its usual purple.

"By all that's holy," he spluttered, "do they not know this is the Siberia of the fur trade! Finlay," he added hastily as Robert continued to scratch across the paper, "there's no need to put that in the letter."

But Mr. Connolly's anger had little effect. I was not at all surprised to hear him storming into the warehouse, looking for Mr. Douglas, one day in March.

"James, where are you?" he cried. "Do you know what the

rogues have done to me now? Half of the blackguards have handed me their notice to resign, if you please!"

I wondered who would replace them. More like Gaston? Mr. Connolly had apparently had the same thought, for, catching sight of me, he said, "You, lad, you can write a fair hand, I hear? Come and set down what I say. If I do it, the Gentlemen will never be able to read it!"

I glowed with the honour of writing the Factor's letter to the Gentlemen of the Company. Soon, having carefully cut a new quill, I was sitting at the Factor's desk with its dozens of tiny pigeonholes stuffed with papers, writing to Mr. Connolly's dictation as he strode up and down the office. The candle flame fluttered in the draught he made in his restless tramping.

"I would beg it as a favour," boomed Mr. Connolly after explaining the mass desertion of the employees, "that no more convicts be transported hither, we have outdoor rogues enough to guard against without having any among ourselves, and I fear that we have already too many of the latter description. And you'll know who I mean," he added, "you and your young friend, won't you, Peter? Blackhearted snake! But you'll not be putting that in the letter, mind."

Once I had sanded the ink, Connolly looked over the letter and grunted his approval. "We'll have you apprenticed yet," he said, folding the letter and sealing it with a big blob of red wax.

The letter had no apparent effect on the Gentlemen in

their remote offices, but the loss of the men was forgotten when another piece of news burst upon the Fort.

James Douglas was going to marry Amelia Connolly!

SIXTEEN

❦

A Spring Wedding

My heart lifted when I heard the news. It seemed to fit the time of year perfectly; the snow was beginning to recede, leaving little islands around the tree roots. The rhubarb behind the men's house was pushing the blind pink snouts of its first shoots into the air and birds were once again singing. I had seen a raven slowly flapping overhead that very morning carrying a large twig in its beak. It was spring!

The wedding was to take place at the end of April. The day before, Cadunda silently reappeared. After supper that night, Robert, looking very pleased with himself, took Cadunda and me into the cabin next to the tradestore where the couple would be married. He told us to carry a ladder and he himself brought a selection of chisels and hammers and knives.

We set the ladder up inside the cabin and held the bottom while Robert climbed. On the face of the squared log over the single door he carved the date, April 27th., 1828, and then two names: James Douglas and Amelia Connolly. It took a long time, but finally Robert set down his tools, wiped his face, which was smeared with lampblack, and surveyed his handiwork from the ground.

"That's our wedding present," he announced, satisfied.

The next day, the men and women and children, Mrs. Connolly, and all her large family crowded into the tiny square cabin. Mr. Connolly, who as Chief Factor had the same powers as the captain of a ship, stood waiting to conduct the ceremony. James Douglas fidgeted nervously.

Finally Amelia entered, a tiny figure dressed in a dark full skirt, a flowered blouse and a bonnet. She looked very grown up, and I remembered with a shock that she was just two years older than I was.

Mr. Connolly read from a battered prayer book. The words had a familiar ring to them.

"Do you, James, take this woman to be your lawful wedded wife?" And when James had stumbled through his responses, he turned to his daughter.

"Do you, Amelia, take this man . . ."

And finally, "By the authority vested in me as Chief

Factor of the Hudson's Bay Company in New Caledonia, I pronounce you man and wife."

And then Cadunda and I were peering between arms at James and Amelia kissing, and Mrs. Benoît was noisily weeping, and the Connollys were all crowding about the couple. When James and Amelia were able to leave, they turned arm in arm to the door and the crowd shuffled aside to let them through.

At the second step, James paused and directed Amelia's attention upwards. Her face lit up as she saw the inscription over the door. Robert beamed in satisfaction at the success of his gift and the murmurs of surprise as everybody saw it.

Work was forgotten for the remainder of the day. There was a grand feast. Mrs. Benoît and Mrs. Connolly surpassed themselves, creating a cake from some carefully hoarded barley flour and dried berries, as well as cooking a mound of bannock and a fine roast dog. I was sad that one of the dogs had been sacrificed, but it was such a rare treat, that after hesitating a little I ate it anyway. At least it wasn't Blaze. He had grown enormously and was now much too valuable a sled dog to be part of the menu.

The men drank the health of the couple in a raspberry-flavoured rum drink called shrub, and night fell to the sound of Benoît's fiddle. The floor was cleared and everyone danced. Even I danced with Amelia. The boatmen were wearing their best deerskin jackets and red sashes and beaded leggings, and they stamped their feet and kicked up their heels like colts while the women danced silently, their eyes on the floor, as the violin and upturned pot someone was using as a drum drove us relentlessly through jig and reel. Some of the Carrier people had been invited to the celebration, too, and Cadunda joined his uncle, Chief Kwah, to watch our antics.

When we were exhausted and slumped, sweating, on the chairs and stools, our eyes smarting as the candles guttered and smoked, it was the turn of the singers. Mrs. Benoît had everyone clapping in time to voyageur songs and by the end of the evening, Mr. Connolly was so affected by singing a melancholy Irish ballad that he made himself weep, and Mrs. Connolly had to thump him on the back and lend him her kerchief to wipe his eyes. This appeared to amaze the Carrier.

I fell asleep that night full of contentment and cake. In a quiet moment during the festivities, Mr. Connolly had informed Robert that it was time I was formally apprenticed to the Company. I thrilled to a future where I would soon be earning the princely sum of fifteen pounds a year. I imagined myself a Clerk, like Robert, then an Officer, a Factor, the Governor, even.

Yes, Governor of the Hudson's Bay Company. Why not? And I would have an excellent opportunity of seeing first hand what it took to be the most important man in the Company. The other piece of news that Mr. Connolly had sprung on us was that Sir George Simpson, the Governor himself, was coming on a visit to Fort St. James that very year!

Tzoelhnolle could not have seemed more remote.

SEVENTEEN

๑

Mr. Douglas Takes Charge

Summer burst upon the Fort in a welcome riot of heat and sparkling light. The days grew longer and longer until the sun barely set at all; at eleven o'clock at night there would still be a luminous glimmer through which the bats darted and wheeled.

My day started at four in the morning, but early rising in the pearly light was effortless compared to squirming into my clothes under the covers, then stumbling out of my narrow cot and breaking the ice in the water jug before I could wash in the aching cold of winter.

I was helping Mr. Douglas to sort a heap of beaver pelts, separating the kits and making two other piles for large and medium furs, when Mr. Connolly loomed in the doorway.

"Well, James," he announced, "I'm away then. Lord knows, we're short handed and it's no time to be removing myself, but orders are orders. If the weather holds, I'll make good time to Fort Fraser. Look for me in a month. I'll be back well before His Holiness gets here, don't worry. And if there are any problems, you can always call on Waccan. He's a grand lad to have at your back in a brawl."

James Douglas nodded seriously.

"Leave it to me," he said. "Enjoy your trip. You don't have to worry about a thing."

The two men left the warehouse and I could hear the thumping of feet on the dock and the muted splashing of paddles and the shouted farewells as Mr. Connolly's canoe slid out onto the lake. Then Douglas was back, rubbing his hands briskly, looking eager and secretly gleeful. Why, I thought, he's like a little boy left alone in the house with all those things he's been told not to touch!

"Hop to it, Peter," Douglas commanded, "no time to let your wits go woolgathering."

Apparently James Douglas was determined to use this opportunity to establish his reputation as a hard taskmaster. The next few days passed in a blur of work and exhaustion as Douglas whipped up the men, goading them on, setting them to mending and making repairs about the Fort even when they had done their work for the day. There was no slackening.

"The Devil finds work for idle hands," he said firmly when Robert ventured to suggest a brief rest.

All the time, Douglas fizzed with energy and confidence. Only once did this falter. A week after Mr. Connolly left, an Indian came to the Fort and sought out Waccan. The Indian was not a local Carrier; it seemed he had come from the Babine Lake area. He and Waccan had a long conversation in the unfamiliar dialect, then the Indian went and sat on the ground outside the gates.

Waccan put on his broad brimmed hat and stumped over the creaking floorboards of the tradestore office where Douglas was working on the accounts. I was sweeping the floor in the store itself and eavesdropped shamelessly.

Waccan's face was bleak.

"I have to leave," he said baldly.

Douglas looked up and waited for an explanation, but Waccan was silent. The two men stared at each other until Douglas broke the silence.

"For what reason?" he asked. "It would have to be very pressing."

"Is murder pressing enough?"

Douglas stared. "Who? What do you mean?"

"My half-brother, Duncan Livingstone, has got himself killed out at Babine Lake. I must go."

"But what good can you do? He will be buried long before you arrive."

"Burial? I'm not concerned with burial! It's revenge I want!"

Douglas fidgeted with his quill pen. His face was anxious.

"Be careful," he said. "It would be a disaster to upset the Indians, especially now, when the Governor's coming, and that other business at Fort George is still on the books."

"It would be even more disastrous not to repay those devils in kind! What kind of message would that send? What mischief would that encourage them to work for the Governor, eh?"

Douglas nodded.

"You have a point," he agreed. "Be diplomatic, though. We want no trouble."

Waccan smiled grimly.

"I'll be diplomatic," he said. "I'm well known for my diplomacy," and with that he slammed his clenched fist on the desk as he turned to go. He passed me without a glance. I watched him go, feeling almost sorry for the Babine Indians with this vengeful whirlwind bearing down on them. Waccan was part Indian, of course, so I understood his instinct for revenge, but it was still murder, wasn't it? Could murder, even as punishment for murder, ever be lawful? And was such violence the right way for the Company to stay in control and keep its business going? When there were so few of us and so many Indian people, did it make any sense to anger them?

Perhaps I was not the only one struggling with a dilemma. As I turned back to my broom, I saw that James Douglas was gnawing his bottom lip, still watching the retreating figure through the dusty window where a trapped bluebottle buzzed helplessly against the parchment.

Douglas looked young and small, suddenly, and very lonely. A great weight was bowing his shoulders and bending his spine.

I hoped fervently that nothing would happen in the next few weeks.

∽

EIGHTEEN

A Secret Message

Once again my useless hands slid helplessly down the walls of my tomb in a hail of loose stones, and I reared gasping out of my dream.

For a moment I sat, confused, my panting loud in the still room. Gradually my heartbeat slowed and my eyes adjusted to the dark. I recognized the shape of the antlers on the wall that held my hat and coat and the rough wooden chair on which my shirt hung, its sleeves trailing to the floor as if exhausted. The wolf skin that served as a rug lay flat between the beds, its dried prune nose pointing at the door.

The dogs were howling and yapping outside. I shivered.

Cadunda always said that dogs barked at ghosts and the spirits of the dead.

I judged that it was nearly dawn but it was much too dark to see the face of Mr. McDougall's watch. Robert was a gently snoring hump on the other side of the room.

"It was just a dream," I told myself as I had a hundred times before, lying down again and pulling up the ground-hog robe I used as a blanket. It had somehow become trapped under my body, binding my arms as effectively as a straitjacket.

But in spite of telling myself there was nothing to fear, sleep eluded me. I lay listening to the dogs and Robert's muffled snorts, and the minutes stretched out as the dawn crept up and the things in the room gradually shook off their disguise and assumed their familiar shapes.

Eventually the dogs fell silent and I heard Mrs. Benoît downstairs stirring the fire. It was a relief to get up and pad about on the wolfskin rug, dressing hurriedly for breakfast.

Down in the kitchen, I collected my ration of fish from Mrs. Benoît. I looked for a space at the big table as far away from Gaston as possible, but I still had to pass the man because he was sitting at the end.

Gaston was shovelling fish into his mouth as if his plate was about to be snatched away. He looked absorbed in his food, but as I rounded his chair, a foot shot out and hooked my ankle, and before I knew it, I was sprawling full length on the kitchen floor, my head resting on a pillow of fish and the blue enamel plate turning cartwheels under the chair legs.

There was a shout of laughter, led by Gaston, who added insult to injury by tenderly helping me up and brushing me down, with little bruising whacks.

"Oh, oh, *mon Dieu*," said Gaston, "a bad case of dropsy! You need a doctor, you think?"

At that moment a dog nipped smartly through the open door, seized the fish and disappeared. A great shout went up from the table, and Gaston joined in.

"*Dommage*," he said, "but don't worry. Now you won't have to clean the floor and Madame, she won't bang your ears for you!"

The day, begun badly, got worse. For the whole morning, I worked in the garden. I hoed row after row of potatoes and turnips. I noticed that many of the turnip tops were covered with tiny white flies; the last time that had happened, we had lost the entire crop.

Lunch was more fish. The sun climbed higher and higher; the Company flag hung limply on the flagstaff. The afternoon promised nothing but more drudgery, cutting poles and digging post holes to mend gaps in the palisade. I thought enviously of Cadunda. On a day like this my friend would be out fishing or hunting.

The afternoon passed in a blur: my hands stuck with slivers from the raw posts as if I had tangled with porcupines; sweat dripping from the end of my nose, stinging my eyes and caking the dust in every fold of skin; mosquitoes and blackflies crowding in to feast; my shoulder muscles popping and snapping with the strain of lifting the heavy posts and hammering them in to the stony soil; James Douglas losing his temper, shouting, "That's not straight! Take it out! Do it again!"

By evening I wanted nothing more than the chance to slip out of the crowded men's house where Gaston and his cronies were playing cards and filling the low-ceilinged room with smoke from their clay pipes. I found a spot by the palisade, in the shadow of the bastion with its tiny cannon, and waited for the breeze to cool me. I was startled by a sudden whisper. It came from the other side of the palisade, close to the ground.

"'Atsul nyulhyatisduk 'et huwa soozílhts'ai," I heard. "Listen, because I am going to talk to you."

It was a girl's voice. It sounded familiar. Could it be Cadunda's sister? I twisted round to hear better.

"I am to tell you the man you want is here. In the village."

"What man?" I asked.

"The man you want. Here, in the village. Tzoelhnolle."

My heart jumped at the name.

"The murderer?"

"The man you want, I am to say."

"Where in the village is he hiding?"

But there was no reply.

I scrambled to my feet, ran to the Officers' house and

hammered on the door. Mr. Douglas' young wife opened it and looked enquiringly at me.

"Oh, Amelia," I began, from long habit, then stopped in confusion. Amelia might be no more than fifteen, only two years older than me, but she was now a married lady. "Mrs. Douglas, ma'am, excuse me, could I have a word with Mr. Douglas? It's very important," I added, seeing her hesitate.

"What do you want?" James Douglas said sternly as he came to the door. Amelia hovered just behind him. She nodded at me encouragingly.

"Mr. Douglas, sir, I was sitting by the palisade, all by myself, and someone — a girl, I think, I couldn't see her — spoke to me from the other side."

"What the devil!" Douglas snorted. "Why d'you think I'd be interested in your little conversations with your sweetheart?"

"No, no," I protested, and Amelia came to my rescue.

"Now, James," she murmured, "give the boy a chance. He wouldn't have come unless it was important."

"Mmm," said Douglas, doubtfully. "Well, get on with it, then. And make it good!"

I began again.

"The girl had a message. She'd been *sent* by someone in the Carrier village, I'm sure."

"And?"

"The message was, that the man we wanted is in the village."

"That's all? That doesn't mean much, does it? What man?"

I was amazed that Mr. Douglas did not leap immediately to my own conclusion. How could he forget that the Company was still looking for a murderer?

"Don't you see?" I urged. "She must have meant Tzoelhnolle! He must have come to the village secretly. Perhaps the chief doesn't really want him there, either."

James Douglas stared at me, his fingers nervously jangling the keys in his pocket. His forbidding expression had gone and he looked young and eager.

"That makes sense, James," Amelia added. "I don't think Kwah would want to anger the Company by sheltering such a man close by, even if he couldn't bring himself to hand him over. He wants his own hands to stay clean."

"Well," Douglas declared, "I can oblige him in that!"

A thought struck him.

"But tell me, Peter," he said, "how do you know what the message was? Don't tell me this girl was chattering to you in English! How do I know you're not just making it up?"

"I do understand some of the Carrier language, sir," I replied with what I hoped was dignity. "My friend has taught me. I may not know as much as Waccan, but I can make myself understood!"

"Oh, oh," laughed Douglas. "Hurt pride, I see. Well, well, Waccan had better watch out. He's got a rival for his job!"

"Stop your teasing, James," Amelia murmured.

"You're right, my dear," her husband said fondly. "You did well to tell me," he added, turning to me. "There's our task for the morning! We've got him! At last!"

Then he turned to Amelia and chuckled gleefully, "And won't your father be pleased!"

Douglas seemed to have forgotten his own advice to Waccan. His eyes sparkled with enthusiasm. I thought he looked exactly like the trappers when they finally got the better of some wily animal like a wolverine, which had eluded them for months, broken their traps, stolen or spoiled their catch, and made them, with all their cunning, look like fools.

Amelia, though, had a thoughtful look on her face as she closed the door.

◎

NINETEEN

Tzoelhnolle

Next day, routine was abandoned. Mr. Douglas rallied the men outside the tradestore.

"Now's our chance to square accounts!" he cried. "Confound his impudence, showing his face here. As if we'd ever forget! Arm yourselves, all of you, and we'll see to a little justice!"

Robert looked doubtful.

"You'll not be needing the lad for this business, sir?" he suggested.

Douglas swept the implied objection aside.

"Peter can carry extra weapons. Besides, he's the only one who has ever seen Tzoelhnolle. You don't want us seizing the wrong man, do you?"

And waving an old blunderbuss, Douglas led his small band, armed mainly with garden hoes and rakes, out of the gates towards the Indians' summer village. Robert was left behind to look after the store.

I trailed along, clutching a heavy mattock and an adze. Now that the moment had come I wished I was almost anywhere rather than the shore of Stuart Lake, fast approaching the village where the hunted man waited. Dread mixed with a queasy excitement turned my stomach to jelly and froze my blood. I was shivering despite the heat of the sun. Perhaps, I hoped, Kwah and his men would stop us and we could turn round and go home.

The village was almost deserted. The men had gone hunting and there were just a few women and children, who watched us silently but made no move to hinder us.

"Split up!" Douglas shouted. "Search everything. Don't leave a thing unturned! And sing out when you find him!"

He stormed about the encampment, and the men, taking their cue from him, overturned baskets and fish racks, tore down lines and nets, invaded every tent, until one uttered a cry of triumph as he pulled aside a pile of fur blankets.

A man holding a bow was cowering behind the furs.

At first, I did not recognize him. The man looked shrunken, much smaller than I remembered. In the pale dusty face the dark eyes darted restively to and fro like agitated mice. The energy, the gleaming malice that had tried to choke the life out of me, that swung the dreadful axe in my dream, was no longer there. Had I imagined it, in my terror? Had Tzoelhnolle simply been driven distracted by my sudden appearance in that woodshed long ago, and taken the obvious way to stifle me? Had he been as appalled as I? He looked far more pathetic than dangerous now, hugging the ground behind the toppled furs. I remembered suddenly hearing Robert and Benoît talking about the woman who had been the cause of the quarrel. Had she been grateful, I wondered, to be snatched back by this man? Had they been happy together or had his life been a misery of fear and pursuit ever since?

My thoughts scurried about my skull. I hated to be the one who would actually point the finger of accusation. But the man was a murderer. And if it had been Cadunda who had tried in his own way to resolve the matter, wouldn't pretending not to know Tzoelhnolle be a betrayal of my friend, as well?

James Douglas was looking at me enquiringly, his eyebrows raised. I took a deep breath and said doubtfully, "Well . . ." trying to delay the moment as long as I could before I was forced to commit myself one way or the other, hoping for something to intervene and relieve me of the responsibility. Tzoelhnolle turned his gaze on me and his pleading eyes widened in what I would have sworn was astonishment. Then his lips curled back exactly like a dog's in a snarl. I took a step back.

"Ah!" crowed Douglas. "Tzoelhnolle, I presume?"

"No," said the man, "no!" but then, quick as a snake striking, he snatched up the bow and an arrow buzzed spitefully past Douglas' ear.

"So the viper has fangs!" Douglas roared and discharged his blunderbuss pointblank at the murderer. The old weapon, which had probably been outdated in the Napoleonic Wars, misfired. Douglas cursed frantically as Tzoelhnolle scrambled free of the furs.

"Go to it, men! After him!"

Now Gaston led the attack. With an oath, and hacking savagely with his hoe, he lunged at Tzoelhnolle, who was desperately fumbling another arrow to his bowstring. The blows gave a silent permission. Others joined him, slowly at first, then more energetically, until at last they were frenzied in their haste to finish and have done. I hung back, watching the arms rising and falling as if in a dream. The hoes swung and I remembered the soft chop as I decapitated weeds the day before, the green ooze that smeared the blade, and listened to the sickening sounds as the very same tools hit their human target. My breath came shallow and very fast, and I felt sick. Benoît, I noticed, was holding back, too. I wondered if my own face had the same extraordinary green pallor.

It was over quickly. The body lay still and the men stood around it, leaning on their tools, breathing heavily. Douglas was pale and his voice was strained, but he barked orders, and the men dragged the corpse away from the encampment and left it. Scrawny dogs followed with interest; the women and children watched us go, their faces completely expressionless. I found it impossible to meet their eyes.

Back at the Fort, the men remained quite silent, as if the rage that had fired them had flickered out. Perhaps they, like me, knew with sickening conviction that the matter could not possibly rest there, and that they had condemned themselves to a nervewracking wait for the next move in the game.

James Douglas, though, was feverishly energetic. He drove the men, commanding some to fetch a cannon from one of the bastions, others to clear the counter in the tradestore of its brass scale and ledgers so that the weapon could be mounted there, facing the door. He organized powder and shot, and collected all the tools that might serve as weapons and leaned them against the counter.

Finally, he nodded, satisfied, and said, "Let them come. We'll be ready!"

❧

TWENTY

Revenge and the Great Chief Kwah

And come they did. At the time I was perched on the palisade, acting as lookout. The sight of the band of men approaching made me gasp. At their head strode Kwah, the Great Chief. The anger on his face convinced me, if I had needed convincing, that invading the village had been a mistake. I leaped down to warn the others.

"Mr. Douglas!" I yelled, bursting into the tradestore, "They're coming! Loads of them!"

A few of the men flicked frightened faces in my direction, but Douglas took no notice. He herded the men into place and stood in front of the counter, backed by a human wall. I am not ashamed to say I made myself as small as possible in a corner. I wondered if everybody felt as terrified as I did. Robert whispered urgently in my ear.

"Don't try to be a hero," he said. "If it comes to fisticuffs, keep out of the way, d'you hear?"

Mr. Douglas had other ideas, however. He called me to his side.

"Stay here," he whispered. "I need to know exactly what they say, you understand?"

Without warning, the doorway darkened with jostling brown bodies. I caught sight of Cadunda beside Kwah and my heart sank. This was what we had both feared. How could I treat Cadunda as an enemy?

Douglas broke the silence.

"What are you doing here, Kwah?"

Cadunda translated. Douglas glanced at me and I nodded. The translation was accurate.

The Chief's deep voice was measured and grave.

"By what right did you come to my village?" he asked in his own language. "I have no quarrel with the death — a death pays for a death — but by what right did you defile our homes?"

Once again Cadunda translated and Douglas' mouth opened, but the Chief gave him no chance to reply.

"For the insult there must be payment. Pay us, give us gifts, or we take revenge."

I shuddered. I had learned from Cadunda how remorseless the Carrier could be in pursuit of vengeance. He had told me stories of whole families wiped out in such vendettas, of survivors spending years in exile, trying to outlive those who would kill them. Even Kwah had spent years in his youth far from home, trying to stay alive.

James Douglas stiffened. He looked, I thought, like the little terrier Mr. McDougall had kept for a while, which yapped provocatively at the sled dogs from a safe distance for months, until a coyote snapped it up one dark night.

"Pay you?" he said. "Pay you? I am as like to pay a fox for stealing a hen!"

When they heard Cadunda's translation the Indians growled and surged forward. Kwah abruptly pushed me aside, seized Douglas by both arms and grappled with him. It was like a signal. Instantly, men on both sides closed on one another. The quiet store rang with the sounds of scuffling, shouts of fear and pain, muffled oaths and grunts of effort as men flailed and wrestled grimly.

I was ignored for the moment, which suited me very well as you may imagine, for with the best will in the world, a thirteen-year-old boy is no match for a grown man. I looked about me to see if anyone was in need of help.

Robert had his opponent's arm twisted up behind his back and was just running him headfirst into the nearest wall. Benoît's face was smeared with blood which seemed to be pouring from his nose and dripping from the point of his chin, but he had apparently winded his assailant by driving a fist deep into his stomach. The man was doubled up, wheezing like a broken bellows. Waccan's oldest son was not doing so well, either. His long hair was firmly in the grip of his adversary and he was straining to free himself and keep his feet. I decided he needed a hand.

As I squeezed through the turmoil, I suddenly found myself face to face with Cadunda. For a second we stared bleakly at each other. Then a faint smile twitched at Cadunda's mouth and both of us would have turned away, but at that very moment a brawny arm circled Cadunda's throat from behind. Gaston was also seizing an opportunity for revenge!

Two struggling men blundered in front of me. I couldn't reach my friend! I saw Cadunda's face growing dark and fear leaping into his eyes. He was struggling desperately to escape, his fingers prying at Gaston's sleeve, but the man was dragging him backwards off balance and that muscular arm was choking off his supply of air.

I had no time to think. Cadunda's struggles were already weakening. My hand reached blindly towards the garden tools stacked behind the counter and closed on a pitchfork handle. Without a second thought I stabbed at Gaston and heard the howl of pain as the prongs sank hungrily into the back of his meaty thigh.

Cadunda sagged, choking, out of Gaston's grasp. I let the pitchfork clatter to the floor, causing Gaston to howl once more, and, locking my arms round my friend's chest, heaved him to safety behind a barrel full of traps. He was a dead weight. His head lolled against the wall. I could not tell if he was breathing.

"Cadunda!" I shouted, shaking his arm. "Speak to me!"

His eyes opened blearily.

"You're alive!" I crowed.

There was a grin, but as he tried to answer, an expression of pain came over his face and he clutched at his throat.

"Don't talk," I said. "Stay still while I see what's going on."

I peered cautiously over the top of the barrel. Gaston was writhing on the floor and shrieking, while Lizotte, one of his few friends, hauled on the pitchfork, trying to remove the tines from his leg. Robert had just flung his own adversary to the ground and was forcing his way through the throng to Benoît, whose head was being thumped repeatedly against the wall. Robert caught sight of me and gave me a quick wink and nod of approval.

But the battle was not going at all well.

To my horror, Kwah had forced Douglas down on the counter and had a wicked-looking knife pressed against his throat. His followers were crowded around him, howling, urging him on. I was close enough to see the dent the knife was making in Douglas' skin; even as I watched, fascinated, a thin red thread ran from the point of the blade to stain the white shirt and disappear in the Clerk's curly hair.

Kwah's son was shouting triumphantly.

"*Yuzulhghé! Yuzulhghé!* He is killing him!"

I leaped to my feet.

"*'Edineh iloh!*" I screamed. "Don't do it!"

But my protest was drowned in the roar of approval from Kwah's followers, who bellowed louder and louder as if the sound alone could force the knife deeper. In the stifling din, those men from the Fort who were still conscious were frozen like the victims of a spell, holding their breath to arrest the sliding knife.

I watched, transfixed.

❧

TWENTY ONE

Amelia Saves the Day

S uddenly, two small figures in long skirts darted into the store. Amelia, and her friend Nancy, Waccan's wife, alerted by the noise, had dashed to join the fray.

The two young women sized up the situation at a glance. They hurled themselves into the shrieking mass, and fell on Kwah, tugging at his arms, trying to drag him off the prostrate form of James Douglas. At the same time, Amelia was shouting commands, almost as if she were trying to control a large, unruly dog.

"Stop!" she yelled. "Stop! Let go of him this minute! Don't you dare! I won't let you!"

Almost contemptuously, as if they were annoying flies,

Kwah shrugged her aside, and Nancy as well.

"*Scha' talhdóh díni 'et ninẕún ch'ulyaz?*" he chuckled.

His followers roared with laughter and jeered, pointing derisively at the two women. I looked at Cadunda.

"What did he say?" I whispered.

"He said, 'So you say you think you can beat me?'" Cadunda croaked.

I could see why the Carrier thought that was funny in the circumstances.

Briefly, the women conferred, darting desperate glances around the store as they spoke.

"That's no good," Amelia muttered. "We've got to think of something that's more appealing than cutting James' throat. Come on, Nancy, quick! Think!"

"Ohhh, I don't know!" Nancy wailed. "A present! *Buy* them off or something!"

"What with?" asked Amelia. "What do I have? I've got nothing they'd want."

Both women were looking wildly about the store as if the solution might be lurking somewhere in a shadowy corner if they could only spot it among the milling bodies. Nancy's eye was even roving about the ceiling. Suddenly her hand clutched at Amelia's arm as she pointed at the stairs.

"The stock!" Amelia cried triumphantly.

The next minute, Nancy and Amelia were treading on my feet and climbing over Cadunda in their haste to get upstairs.

"Peter, come and help," Amelia panted. "We've got to distract them!"

I stumbled up the stairs after them.

The howling and shouting below was rising to fever pitch.

"Get those blankets," ordered Nancy, as she tore at boxes of tobacco. Amelia was already pitching capots and moccasins down on top of the struggling men. I scooped up a great armful of the thick woollen blankets with the broad coloured stripes along the edge. Soon the three of us were hurling a rain of goods — cloth, leather, babiche, tobacco twist, blankets — onto astonished upturned faces and the howls were diminishing.

Kwah straightened up. Slowly he returned his knife to his belt. There were murmurs of disappointment at this which he quelled with a raised hand. He reached out and picked up a stout wool jacket from the pile of goods littering the counter.

"*Nohni dune 'uht'oh tubeh dahzóo,*" he said at last. "You people are very kind."

I felt Amelia, hanging over the top of the stairs beside me, let out her long-held breath in a great gasp of relief. James Douglas sat up sheepishly.

The Indians growled their approval and surged forward to collect the goods. In no time at all, it seemed, they had stripped the floor and counter, and laden with gifts, had vanished like smoke through the open door. I peered down at the barrel that had sheltered my friend and me. Cadunda had disappeared with the rest of them.

There was nervous laughter. Nancy sat down hard. James Douglas looked up at his wife.

"Amelia," he said slowly, "how am I going to account for all the goods to your father?"

"I don't know, James," Amelia replied. "How would we have accounted for your death?"

James Douglas nodded. Bestirring himself shakily, he ordered me to tidy the store. Robert was helping Benoît, who had a monstrous egg-shaped lump on his head, to his feet. Gaston was still moaning in a corner, clutching his leg, and bleeding profusely. Two men were delegated to carry him off to the men's house and bind up his wound with bear grease.

"Useless idler," snapped Douglas. "I suppose he'll have to be shipped out with the returns in the fall. How will we get a replacement?"

I could not help feeling glad that Gaston would not be staying. Obviously, it was not just the Carrier who took revenge seriously!

As I swept and put the store to rights, I thought about all that had happened. The dogs had been right; there had been ghosts about. Tzoelhnolle had been as good as dead the minute he had stolen into the village. Thank goodness, I thought, I shall never have to dream about him again.

But what about my friendship with Cadunda? Could that ever be the same?

I had my answer that evening. I was standing on the lakeshore, feeling strangely flat after all the excitement of the day. I was watching two loons shepherding their tiny chick between them, when Cadunda appeared in his silent way. For a moment we just looked at each other. Then Cadunda held up the line of willow twine and the bone hook he was carrying.

"*Hukwa'ninzun de sghude'onyaih,*" he said and turned away.

I smiled, relieved. What Cadunda had said was, "You can come with me if you want to."

I did.

❡

TWENTY TWO

The Governor Arrives

I was bent over, carefully laying an armful of marten pelts under the press, when my ears caught a strange sound. I straightened up and listened carefully. It was a melancholy wailing, like an animal in pain, growing and ebbing as if the wind were blowing it to and fro like the heavy folds of the Company flag. Yet it could not be an animal, unless animals sang, for the sound had a swinging rhythm, and as I listened intently, I could just make out the pattern of a melody.

"Robert," I called, "listen. What is that?"

Robert stopped rustling through the tally of furs.

"Why," he said, "that's the sound of the pipes!"

His face stilled as he concentrated and then brightened with a delighted, incredulous smile.

"*Si coma leum codagh na shea!*" he breathed. "It's the march of the clans!"

I was used to Robert coming out with snippets of Gaelic, but I had never heard this one before.

"What does it mean?" I asked.

"It means 'Peace, or war, if you will it otherwise'. It means someone important is coming, a Scot, no doubt."

I looked at Robert, light dawning.

"Could it be Sir George Simpson's arrived? Could it be the Governor already?"

"Only one way to find out! Come on, laddie!"

We both rushed out of the warehouse. Benoît had beaten us to the palisade. He was already leaning over the top of the fence, waving his hat and shouting.

"*C'est le Gouverneur!*" he yelled as he gave me a hand up. "*Regardez!*"

I gazed into the distance, and there, coming slowly down a small hill to the edge of the grey water, was a strange cavalcade.

At the front strode a figure dressed in buckskins, the fringed leather swinging with every step. The man carried a pole with the British Ensign fluttering from it. Behind him came a splendid figure; a man in full Highland dress, his tartan brave in the sun, playing bagpipes. He was followed by two buglers; I could see the flashes as they raised the brass instruments to their lips. After the band rode a single horseman, a dark shape at that distance, with a black hat. He had a train of two more riders, and then came a long line of men, some of them straggling, bent under huge packs. They looked like a procession of turtles. I counted twenty of them. They were followed by a laden packhorse. At the rear were two more figures on horseback, and I thought I could detect that one of them was wearing a skirt and bonnet.

"What the devil are you men up to?"

We all turned at the roar. James Douglas was standing below us, hands on hips. Robert explained. It was almost comical to see the change in Douglas' expression as rage gave way to a startled panic.

"Well, come down!" he shouted. "Fetch the others! Benoît, see to the cannon! Every man to arm himself. We want a volley to welcome the Governor — he's not to think we don't know what's fitting. And give it your all, now — we don't do things by halves at Fort St. James!"

And he ran to the Officers' house to fetch his frockcoat.

Stirred by all the commands and the skirling of the pipes coming closer and closer, the men hurried to the palisade. Benoît and Robert climbed the bastion and huddled over the tiny cannon, pouring the powder carefully, ramming it with the wadding down the barrel. Mr. Douglas ran back to the gate, flinging it wide open, then turned and waved a white kerchief at Benoît. Robert primed the cannon, then turned aside, his fingers in his ears, while Benoît lowered the linstock with its slow match to the touch hole. There was a puff of smoke and a loud boom, followed by a ragged volley of shots as the men on the walls fired their shotguns and small arms into the air.

The volley thundered out again, and again, as James Douglas walked out to meet the cavalcade in front of the Fort.

The men on the palisade cheered as the procession halted and the tall man on the lead horse leaned down and shook the Clerk's hand. Then Douglas gestured toward the gates and the procession started again at a leisurely pace, winding slowly inside the walls.

Douglas beckoned furiously to me to take the bridle of the Governor's horse, and as I held the reins and tried to persuade the animal to stand still while Sir George dismounted, I had a close view of the great man.

Simpson was an imposing figure. He was not a giant, but he gave the impression of towering over others. He had a full, red face and tiny, slate grey eyes that seemed to scan vast distances. His hair was white, and so was his linen. I had never seen anyone who had been travelling for as long as the Governor with such a crisp and snowy shirt and stock. In addition, the Governor wore a sober black suit and a dark curly brimmed beaver hat.

As Simpson levered himself out of the saddle, I stared at the hand resting on the pommel a few inches from my nose. It was a square, capable hand powerful enough for hard labour, but it emerged gracefully from the white frill at the wristband of the sleeve, the skin smooth and clean, the fingernails regular and slightly shiny with clear half-moons, and the little finger heavy with a gold signet ring decorated with curly copperplate initials. I looked down at my own dirty paw, dry and cracked, the nails split and black with grime. Embarrassment made me edge my sleeve over it as far as I could. I have a way to go, I thought, before I can be a Governor.

Simpson turned to Douglas.

"Is this a trustworthy boy?" he asked.

"Certainly, sir."

The Governor looked directly at me.

"Then look after my horse, lad. He deserves only the best."

As I led the bay gelding away, determined to give it the royal treatment, I heard Simpson ask another question.

"And where is Mr. Connolly?"

Douglas hastily explained that he was expecting Connolly back at any time and that the Fort had managed very well in his absence.

"Ah, yes, that reminds me," Sir George continued, "what's this I've been hearing about fisticuffs with the Indians?"

Douglas looked glum as he followed the Governor into the Officers' house but he had an unexpected reprieve from explanations.

A shout from Benoît, still swabbing the cannon on the bastion, turned all heads in his direction.

"I see Mr. Connolly, sir!"

And Connolly it was, travel-stained and weary, stepping out of a canoe on the lakeshore and surrounded by a small band of Carrier, chattering excitedly.

They melted away as Douglas and Simpson and a straggling group of men approached the newcomer. Once again, there were greetings and handshakes and a noisy procession into the Fort, packs to be unloaded and men lodged. Once again, the traveller had an urgent question on his mind.

Even where I was, at the far side of the compound, turning the Governor's horse into the small pasture, I could hear Connolly's booming voice.

"Saints alive, James! What's this you've been at? Starting a war while I'm gone, is it?"

I felt almost sorry for James Douglas.

TWENTY THREE

૭

Setting the Stage

By the next morning, the Governor had learned everything there was to know about the confrontation between Kwah and Douglas. I was summoned abruptly to the
parlour of the Officers' house, where I found myself facing
Simpson and Connolly, both seated in comfortable chairs,
while a hangdog Douglas stood uneasily behind them,
blocking the light from the tiny window overlooking Mrs.
Connolly's few flowers. Even though it was summer, a fire
burned in the big stone fireplace, black with soot, and the
reflection of the flames twinkled cheerfully in Mrs.
Connolly's ornaments: brass candlesticks and trivet, long
stemmed glasses on the sideboard and a heavily beaded

leather pouch containing spills for lighting pipes and candles hanging from the mantel. The Governor broke the silence.

"It's a bad business," said Simpson, "but there's a chance now to settle the matter once and for all. Laddie, they tell me you have a friend in the Carrier village, one of Kwah's kin."

"I do, sir," I replied, "his name's Cadunda."

"And would this Cadunda, d'you think, help you to take a message from me to the chief?"

I hesitated.

"I think so, sir," I said slowly. "I haven't seen much of him since that day, but I don't think he bears a grudge."

"Well, here's what I want you to do. It's my purpose to talk to the chief and set the matter straight. But first I have to get him here. I fancy he won't take kindly to an order, so you must choose your words. Make it a request, if you please, but I'll take no refusal. Maybe your friend can smooth your way and translate for you, if need be. I'd send someone older, but the Interpreter is away, I hear. Now, do you think you can manage this for me?"

I was not at all sure that I could, but I would have died rather than admit it.

"Of course, sir," I said.

"Then off with you. Tell Kwah I'll be waiting for him at noon."

The Governor turned to the other two men.

"Come on, gentlemen," he said, "we have a show to put on."

I hurried along the dark cave of the hallway past the stuffed eagle and the smells of baking and raced to the Carrier village, my mind in turmoil. It was an honour to carry out the Governor's wishes, but suppose I failed? What would happen if Cadunda wouldn't help me? If Kwah simply refused to see me? I had just one trump card.

I made my way quickly to Cadunda's lodge, trying hard not to be discouraged by the unwelcoming faces I passed on my way. Even the dogs seemed hostile, darting out from between the tents, abandoning tussles over fish tails, or standing stifflegged in my path with their hackles rising, barking deep in their throats. I was glad to reach my friend's home. Cadunda was bent over a small hollowed stone, grinding what looked like pieces of some root with another stone shaped to fit his hand. He looked surprised to see me. I quickly explained why I was there.

"So, will you take me to your uncle?" I asked. "Say you will. Don't you see, if there's a meeting with the Governor, and everyone agrees, all this revenge business can stop. Isn't it worth a try?"

Cadunda thought for a minute, then turned to his mother who was sitting quietly lacing snowshoe frames with babiche. He spoke rapidly to her in Carrier. She listened without comment, then nodded.

Cadunda turned to me.

"Come on," he said. "I'll take you to my uncle's lodge."

I left the negotiations to Cadunda. Outside Kwah's lodge, which was bigger than all the others, several of his sons were lounging. They stiffened as we approached and blocked the entrance. Cadunda launched into another explanation in Carrier, urging them to step aside.

One of the young men, the one who had smirked and angered Mr. McDougall when Kwah brought the fish after the murders, folded his arms and turned to his companions.

"*Daja ní whe 'útni?*" he asked, raising his eyebrows in mock bewilderment. "What does he mean?"

Then his hand flew to his mouth as if he had just understood.

"*Duneyaz oobeni hoolil!*" he cried.

"What is he saying?" I whispered.

"Oh, he's just calling me insane," Cadunda replied as the men laughed.

"*Beni hooloh!*" one of the other sons added sourly. His brothers shouted their agreement.

"And stupid," muttered Cadunda.

"*Daja ní?*" came a deep voice from the inside of the tent. The sons stopped laughing abruptly.

"'*Uze!*" called Cadunda. "*Nyoon dune huske-un 'uhoolh-dzin 'eyaíh! Hóonli huwus'a te 'oh totsuk sdulhyóh 'útni!*"

This was beyond me, although I knew that Cadunda had called Kwah's son a miserable, bad-tempered man.

Cadunda looked at me and whispered, "I said he was always fighting and he argues every time I ask him to do something."

"'*Oolníh*," came the voice again. Cadunda smiled and the son looked angry.

"The Chief says his son is jealous," murmured Cadunda.

With a bad grace, the brothers stood aside and allowed us in.

Kwah was sitting cross-legged on a fur blanket in the middle of the floor space. His four wives, each of them busy, occupied the four corners. One was splitting a great coil of spruce root; another was folding fur blankets and making a neat pile of them; the third was wrapping a baby to put it into the little frame she would carry on her back; the fourth was sweeping the dirt floor with a brush made of goose feathers. All the busy hands slowed as the women darted inquisitive glances at us. Kwah greeted Cadunda affectionately and Cadunda talked to him at some length.

"*Khuní nu'a*," my friend said, finally, pointing to me. "He brings a message." Kwah turned to me, with an enquiring look.

"*Ndai la ooka 'ninẓun-i sudóni*," he prompted.

"Tell my uncle just what it is you need," said Cadunda.

I swallowed.

"The Great Chief of the Company sends me with his greetings. He wishes to meet the Great Chief Kwah. He wants to meet the warrior he has heard so much about."

I hoped I could be forgiven for stretching the truth.

"Go on," I said to Cadunda. "Tell him that."

Cadunda translated.

"*Nyoon k'une 'ut'en-un 'aw hoonli hidóni' aít'oh,*" Kwah replied, looking stern.

"What's wrong?" I asked.

"My uncle says the person who does as he likes cannot be told what to do."

"No, no," I said urgently. "It's not a command. It's a *request*. The Governor would *like* him to come to the Fort, but he knows he cannot *command* the Great Chief Kwah!"

I hoped I was not laying it on too thick. My words sounded hopelessly insincere to my own ears, but apparently they pleased Kwah. He spoke directly to me in halting English.

"Tell the Great Chief that Kwah will come." He lapsed back into Carrier. "*K'atle sih nda' tot'ás.*"

"We will walk down later," Cadunda translated.

In a great rush of relief, I made my best bow to Kwah.

"Till noon, at the Fort, then," I said.

"*Dzetniz,*" he agreed. Then, as we were pulling aside the skin of the tent at the doorway, he called out again.

"*Ndet lah hukwá'nuzun de 'et sts'únohdilh!*" he said, smiling.

"My uncle likes you," said Cadunda. "He said to come and visit him whenever you want!"

Cadunda accompanied me to the edge of the village and

waved as I left. My heart was a good deal lighter than when I had come. I felt very proud of myself for accomplishing the task Sir George had set me. Perhaps now there was a chance of settling the whole matter peacefully.

At the Fort, I found preparations for the meeting well advanced. I began to understand what Simpson had meant by putting on a show.

The open area within the fence had been transformed. Within the hollow square formed by the little grey wooden buildings of the Fort, facing the gates, on a little platform of planks balanced on wooden kegs from the warehouse, was the big armchair I had last seen occupied by Simpson in the parlour that morning. It was flanked on either side by flags on poles stuck into the ground, the Ensign on one side and the Company flag on the other. More chairs had been taken from the Officers' house and the office and ranged alongside. The piper was standing to one side, tuning up his instrument, and the buglers lounged against the fence, ready to spring to attention at a second's notice. The long purple and blue vista down the lake, with the floating islands and the fringe of dreaming hills, provided the perfect backdrop.

I found Mr. Connolly and the Governor enjoying a glass of brandy in the cramped tradestore office as they listened to Waccan's account of his adventures at Babine Lake. His canoe had slipped back to the wharf soon after I had left that morning and since then he had been enthusiastically entertaining the visitor with the tale of how he had cornered his brother's murderer and held off a horde of the man's relatives while exacting his revenge. His eyebrows shot up as I reported my conversation with Kwah. I basked in Simpson's approval.

"Well done, lad," rumbled the Governor. "We'll have to send you off as ambassador to foreign parts. Now we just wait for the curtain to rise! Mind you get a good seat for yourself!"

Just before noon I found myself a perch on the palisade. The enclosure lay before me like a stage and I had a grand-stand view. The actors started to take their places; the Governor ascended his red velvet throne, flanked by the gentlemen he had brought with him. Mr. Connolly and Mr. Douglas sat with heads together to one side, while all the Company servants massed behind them. Colin Fraser, the piper, paced up and down, playing the march of the clans. Mrs. Connolly, Amelia, Nancy and the other womenfolk made a soft splash of colour where they sat, and the children crouched at their feet, quiet for once.

Suddenly, the Carrier were there. The piper brought his tune to a skirling halt and the air was then filled with another pounding rhythm. In unison, men thumped the small square hide-covered drums decorated with the animal emblems of their clans. A giant heartbeat filled the enclosure. Men and women danced solemnly to its measure and, at their head, came the medicine man with his apprentice, Cadunda, their faces painted with vermillion. Cadunda was blowing swansdown from the palm of his hand up into the air. He looked as if he moved in a tiny local snowstorm.

Behind Kwah, the Carrier filed through the gateway, automatically lining up to face the Governor in the space that had been left empty. They were a sea of fur robes, leather leggings, salmon skin aprons, bear claw necklaces, porcupine quills and eagle feathers and painted faces.

The two buglers, rigid as poles, split the air with a fanfare.

Now, I thought, the play can begin.

❧

TWENTY FOUR

A Pipe of Peace

The Governor allowed the silence after the fanfare to stretch until I wanted to stand up and shout simply to end the strain of it.

"The Company welcomes the Carrier people," Simpson began. "Tell them that."

Waccan stepped forward to translate.

"However," Simpson continued, "the Company is not pleased with their conduct."

My heart sank. The Governor was not going to patch up differences this way!

The deep voice continued, echoed at slow intervals by Waccan's.

"Your leaders have led you astray," he said. "They have sought to make themselves tall in your eyes by ignoring our kindness, pouring scorn on our promises of justice and mercy. They have thought to humble the Company with threats of vengeance."

There was some stirring in the ranks of brown faces as this was relayed by Waccan, who poured all of the Governor's passion into his own translation. The Governor ignored the reaction and continued at some length, scolding the Carrier for their reluctance to help bring the Fort George affair to a satisfactory end, reproaching them for their disloyalty to the Company which had brought them so many benefits.

"Instead," he went on remorselessly, pointing contemptuously at Kwah, "you throw in your lot with the miserable dog who would attack the Fort and offer violence to its Officer. Shame on you, Kwah!"

I gasped at the insult.

At this point, James Douglas leaped forward as if he could not bear to sit still any more.

"Sir!" he cried. "I must protest, sir! You misjudge the chief. But for his restraint, I would be a dead man. I admit it, myself. Without him I would be the victim of my own rashness. We should give him his due, sir, as I do."

There was a swell of approval at these words on both sides. I watched the Governor's reaction. Would he be angry at Douglas contradicting him like that? Then I caught the twitch of the Governor's mouth and the quick hand that concealed it and understood what he was doing.

The Governor was not really angry. He just had to say these things because the Company could never afford to look weak, but he knew what went on. From that moment I was convinced that it would all come right in the end.

And so it did, although I had one more bad moment. The Governor graciously relented in his attack on Kwah personally, allowing that he could not ignore Douglas' defence of the chief, since James was the injured party.

"But," he went on severely, "be sure of this; on the very next occasion that merits it, the total force of the Company will be turned against you, the innocent will go with the guilty, and your fate will be deplorable indeed!"

I gasped again. This contradicted everything that the Company had said before! How was it possible?

Simpson allowed a moment of silence for this to sink in. I expected an angry murmur to swell among the Carrier ranks, but Kwah stood impassive, head high, and his companions were silent. I remembered all of a sudden that this was a performance. The speech and the threat were part of a ritual familiar to both sides. Kwah had asserted himself and made his point in the tradestore; now he was allowing the Governor his turn. Both of them were great actors!

"Now that we have made that clear," Simpson continued in quite a different voice, "the Company wishes to cement its friendship with the Carrier people."

He beckoned an assistant closer. The man was carrying a tray holding glasses of rum and small packets, ready for this moment which had been planned all along. The Governor picked up two of the glasses and handed one to Kwah. They drank, and Kwah spoke, nodding energetically.

"*'Uzóo!*" he said. "It is good!"

Then Simpson gave Kwah the packets of tobacco twist.

The whole crowd relaxed in an outlet of breath. Simpson lit a long-stemmed clay pipe and puffed on it contentedly for a moment before passing it to Kwah. In his turn, Kwah passed it to Douglas. When the chief men among the Indians and the Company officers were all wreathed in smoke, the piper struck up the peace song again.

Without any obvious signal, the ceremonial was at an end. People began to drift off, chattering like the swallows dipping tirelessly overhead. I was left to stare at the great armchair abandoned in the centre of the stockade facing the gate. It no longer resembled a throne; in fact, it looked silly and out of place, as if it had tumbled from some other world above the clouds and landed quite by accident in this quiet clearing by the lake. I felt flat, as you do when excitement is at an end, and my thoughts turned sombre.

What would have happened, I wondered, if Kwah had not been content with nearly frightening Mr. Douglas half to death? If Amelia and Nancy had not been so quickwitted? If Sir George had not smoothed the incident away so diplomatically? Both sides walked away with dignity this time, thanks to these strong characters who tried to do the right thing as they saw it, but supposing there were no Kwahs or Amelias in the future? In sudden bleak understanding, I realized how complicated life had become for Cadunda's people, now that we were there, a different clan, with very different ideas, spreading everywhere and more of us coming all the time. That armchair had landed, and squatted firmly on this alien shore; there was no shipping it back now.

Suddenly Cadunda was by my side. His smile was the same as ever but he looked different, nonetheless. Perhaps it was my way of seeing him that was different. That day I had seen for myself how important he was to his uncle. I had been impressed by his role in the ceremony, even more impressed that the other Carrier people had all apparently accepted his right to it. But now I caught myself wondering how long he could follow the old way. Carrier hunters hung longingly over guns when they came to the tradestore; their womenfolk fingered the blankets and iron pots. Even Cadunda had somehow acquired a boatman's red sash and was wearing it wrapped several times round his lean waist.

"I've come to say goodbye," he said.

"Why?" I asked. "Where are you going?"

He smiled. "No, not me. You. You will be leaving soon."

"That's news to me," I protested. "Where would I go? And how do you know, anyway? I'll be here to pester you for years, you see if I don't!"

He shook his head. "No," he insisted, "our paths go different ways now. My place is here." His gaze followed a flight of ducks angling down to land on the lake, their wings whistling. "Yes," he repeated dreamily, "this is my place. But," he added mischievously, looking directly at me again, "I will not forget what the bear wanted to eat. Poor bear, you would have choked her!"

I punched at his arm and he dodged, laughing.

"Goodbye!" he called, skipping backwards out of reach. He was swallowed up in a passing crowd of young men before I could speak, but I could still see a hand waving over their heads. Slowly, I raised my own arm in salute. My last glimpse of him came as his group joined the Chief. Kwah turned toward the open gate, his followers ranged behind him. I could make out Cadunda's slight form at his uncle's right hand as they left the compound. He did not give a single backward glance. It was at that moment, I think, that I knew he was right; we were destined for very different lives and could not possibly spend them together. Knowing each other, though, had marked us both for ever.

Feeling bereft, I joined the children who were crowding round the piper, watching his fingers flying on the chanter and his cheeks swelling as he squeezed the bag under his arm. He finished the march and launched into a reel that had some of the Company servants kicking up their heels. Those who did not dance stood around clapping their hands to the beat.

Then the Governor joined the circle round the piper. At his heels was his dog, a sleek black hound, quite unlike Blaze and the other sled dogs that lived at the Fort. The Governor twinkled at the children's solemn faces, took out his snuffbox, looked at his dog who sat gazing into his face expectantly, and commanded, "Speak!"

The dog barked gruffly, once.

A pretty tinkling tune immediately started.

The children gasped and jostled each other to see where the music was coming from.

Again the Governor commanded, "Speak!"

The dog barked, and the music stopped. The children pressed close, their mouths open in amazement.

Sir George chuckled, pleased with the effect.

An arm reached for the box but the Governor twitched it aside, laughing and shaking his head, and strolled away, taking a pinch of snuff as he went, his dog close at heel. The children began to drift off, too, talking animatedly, mystified but apparently well pleased. I realised the snuffbox was also a musical box, something I had heard about, but never seen, but I, too, wanted to know how the dog controlled the music. I followed the Governor and his hound.

Timidly, I plucked up the courage to address the great man.

"Sir," I ventured, "your dog is wonderfully clever. How does he make the music play?"

The Governor chuckled.

"Now that would be telling, wouldn't it?"

"But sir, won't you give me a hint?"

The Governor's face became serious. He was no longer teasing.

"Let me give you a little advice, lad," he said. "If I gave away old Tray's secret, you would only feel cheated. When you meet magic, don't be too anxious to find out how it works. It's a bit like taking a clock to pieces — it will never be the same again. And when you *make* magic, always keep something back up your sleeve."

And he gave me a solemn wink as he left.

For some reason, I found myself thinking of Cadunda again.

❦

TWENTY FIVE

Onward

The snuffbox was not the only bit of magic the Governor had up his sleeve.

He spirited the limping Gaston away to McLeod Lake with sorely needed supplies. On his way to Fort St. James, he had stopped there to switch from canoe to horseback and found the Clerk, John Tod, and his two men in desperate straits, pale and thin as rails from eating nothing but berries for two weeks. Gaston was useless for any heavy work, but he could be spared to ride a horse loaded with whitefish, and nobody missed him.

The biggest surprise, though, was the Governor's decision about James Douglas. He announced that Douglas would be going to Fort Vancouver, way down south at the mouth of the Columbia, to act as accountant.

"Perhaps that will keep you out of trouble," he said, "and the Company, too."

Then to my astonishment he summoned me and said, "Time for you to move, too, I think. How would you like to go as apprentice with Mr. Douglas? Are you ready, d'you think?"

I was overwhelmed. Fort Vancouver! I knew it was a great step to go there. So much would be frightening, even dangerous. I would be leaving Robert and Cadunda and Benoît and cosy Mrs. Benoît, everything that I knew, in fact. I would probably never be able to take Chief Kwah at his word and visit him. I would never see Cadunda's mother and sister again, never watch his grandmother pounding roots or stewing bark for her medicines. Life in their village would go on and I would be no part of it, not even in my minor role as Cadunda's friend. The Fort would go on, too. The little Benoîts would grow up, and forget all about the boy who had kept them from falling in the fire when they had started to walk, and stopped their squabbles by tickling them until they were helpless.

I would be exposed, raw, in a strange new world where not even the weather would behave in ways I was used to. There would be strangers, too, unknown quantities who would have no reason to show me tolerance or compassion as Robert had done, no special inclination to help me or excuse my mistakes. Some of them might eventually turn into friends. There was a hollow feeling about my heart, though, at the thought of leaving Cadunda behind. I had found friendship where I had never expected it among a people who were as constant a presence outside the palisade as the lake and the trees, yet, I now realised, even more mysterious.

I had learned much from the boy who had twice saved my skin. It was not just a matter of knowing about animals and birds and fish and plants, the tricks of survival. It was more than picking up the rudiments of another language and knowing the power that gave me.

Cadunda's greatest gift had been his sureness. How he came by it still baffled me; there was more to my friend than met the eye. It made my breath come short at that moment just to think of his farewell. How had he known we were to part? Whatever the truth of that mystery, his certainty and confidence had shown me, far more convincingly than all of Robert's encouragement and Mrs. Benoît's pats and hugs, welcome though they had been, that it was possible for me to stand alone. I no longer trembled at everything, no longer felt the victim of events I could not control. I had shaken off fear and hopelessness, and discovered the power of understanding and loyalty, of diplomacy and magic.

Excitement tingled deep inside me now, small yet, but swelling. I was now an official servant of that Company which held the future, for better or worse, in its hand. Would I ever influence its actions as the Governor, now sitting in front of me looking quizzical, had done? I saw myself with one foot still in an old world, already shrinking in my astonished imagination, the world of Mr. Connolly and Waccan and Gaston, full of simple, brutal rules and vengeful blows. The other foot was already striding into other possibilities.

My mind filled with visions of the river and the sea, which I had never seen, of sailing ships and sailors from the far corners of the earth, of Russian fur traders and fashionable ladies, different Indians with strange ways and unfamiliar tongues to learn and understand. For a moment my fancy dressed me in Sir George's impeccable linen and stylish beaver hat, and I saw myself at the heart of the great enterprise which was the Company, my fingers on all the threads, drawing them close together, helping to make a country where a country had never been, of which even wild, empty New Caledonia could be a part. No place under my rule for club law and vengeance! Instead, I would have Chief Kwah's restraint and the friendly smoke of the peace pipe, and insist on talk rather than blows.

Robert always said my head was forever in the clouds! There I was, already taking over the Governor's job, when I had not even accepted his offer of an apprenticeship, a position so exalted that it would make me almost equal to David, who had still not fattened up sufficiently to be sure of keeping his trousers up.

These thoughts had whirled about my head in seconds, formless scraps that I could never have put into words in the time it took to think them. But my mouth was dry with excitement as I looked at the circle of expectant faces — Mr. Connolly, red and breathing heavily, Mr. Douglas slightly scowling as if I had no business making them wait for a reply, Sir George smiling, one eyebrow raised.

There was only one possible response, of course.

"Oh yes, sir, if you please!" I cried, my eyes shining.

ABOUT THE AUTHOR

Margaret Thompson was born in England and lived there until 1967 when she came to Canada with her husband and two very young sons. A third child, a daughter, arrived a year later.

Writing has always been a passion, but until 1996, most of her time was spent teaching others to write. She was an English teacher in the high schools at Merritt, Madeira Park, Sechelt and Fort St. James, BC, and a part-time instructor for the College of New Caledonia.

With her roots in the Old World, she has always loved and valued history and was able to pursue that interest in northern BC through her long association with the Friends of Fort St. James National Historic Park Society.

In addition, she enjoys animals, especially her nineteen-year-old Siamese cat, birdwatching, gardening, cooking, and her two grandchildren. She likes to travel, especially in Greece, is an omnivorous reader, and has recently rediscovered the ability to knit.

Margaret Thompson has now exchanged six months of snow for year-round gardens, and is living and working in Victoria, BC.